Fifty Shades
of Black & Blue

---

a parody

I B Naughtie

Copyright 2012 by Black and Blue Press

Library of Congress Cataloging-in-Publication Data available on request.

ISBN 978-1-4675-3099-6

Fifty Shades
of Black & Blue

a parody

Chapter One

I can't believe how lame my hair looks. You'd think after three semesters in Beauty School and an advanced certification in Hair Styling I'd be able to do something with my freakin' hair. But NO! Plus this is a really big day for me since I'm taking the bus down to Hoboken for a job interview. Working in the auto parts supply field is not exactly my dream job, but I figure I'll work there until I can save up enough to have my own beauty salon in Jersey City – or at least rent a station at my Aunt Dolores' shop. Meantime, I've got to get this hair under control!

My roommate Shelly is no help. All she does is complain about her boyfriend Victor, who is this big doofus who spends all day lounging on the couch at our apartment looking at pornos. What a creep. I don't get what she sees in him. I tell her "He's a big doofus!" But all she can say is "I know, but I love him." I don't get it. She's got no ambition at all. At least I invested the time and money to go to Beauty School. But Shelly just sits on her fat butt and brings beer to her stupid boyfriend. You'd think she could at least get a job at Taco Bell or something. She actually was supposed to have an interview with this guy who knows this guy who has a job opening. But she didn't feel like going "all the way to fucking Hoboken," so I asked if I could go in her place. She said, "Sure, what the fuck."

Anyways, I am pretty nervous about this interview today. It turns out I'm meeting with the big boss of the whole auto parts supply company, Vincent Griso. Ever since I was a little girl, I heard about Vinnie's Auto Parts. He owns like twenty stores all over Jersey. My pop used to take me there all the time until he ran off with that slut Tina. My mom hired a couple of Puerto Rican guys to find him and beat him up, but they just took the money and spent it on cock fights. After that, my mom got real depressed and gained like seventy-five pounds and started going to church. I think she had a crush on Father Greg, which is sick.

I made it to the bus stop just in time. There are these punks on my corner who hassle every girl who walks by – even dogs like Maureen Tilden. I don't get it with those guys. They don't seem to care what a girl looks like, as long as she's a girl. I mean, I see these girls with no fashion sense it all, dressed in like boring outfits with stringy hair and the guys are all like "Hey, baby, wanna fuck?" I mean, what is with them?

Anyways, I made it past the dumb punks on the corner and got on the bus. I hate the fucking bus. Nothing but old ladies and weirdos. Once I was on the Number 5 and this homeless guy had peed in his pants and was passed out on the seat. It was totally gross. So now I don't look at anybody. I just open up my Cosmo magazine and pretend to be reading. Speaking of Cosmo, what is it with all these skinny fucking girls? They look like skanky junkies to me.

So after about a half-hour, I get off downtown at the world headquarters of Vinnie's Auto Parts. I'm looking for the address and when I come round the corner, I can't believe my eyes. There is this amazing steel and glass building with the Vinnie's Auto Parts logo – a carburetor with a blonde girl in a bikini kind of draped over it – plastered over the front of the building. But the coolest thing was that the building itself was designed to look like an actual carburetor – you know, with the hose coming out of it and everything. How cool is that?

I just stood there for like five minutes staring at the building. Then I realized I was going to be late for my interview so I checked myself out in my hand mirror – ugh! There was nothing I could do about my freakin' hair, but I did an emergency mascara application and slathered on some red lip gloss just as a precaution. Then I straightened my skirt and hiked up my boobs. I was finally ready for my big interview!

So I go into the big carburetor building and there's this security guard there like the place is fucking Fort Knox. Which is very classy, if you ask me. Most places you can just walk in and go to the bathroom and do whatever, but here you've got to sign in and everything.

The guard says "Can I help you?" and I say "I'm here to see Mr. Griso."

And he says "Mr. Griso Senior or Mr. Griso Junior?"

Oh fuck. Double fuck! I didn't know there even was a Mr. Griso Senior or Junior. At this point I'm getting really nervous, so I sort of stick out my lower lip and kind of make my voice soft while I lean over and stick my chest out. "I don't know exactly," I whisper.

That seemed to work great because the security guy smiled and picked up the phone.

"I'll find out for you, honey."

I just smiled back at him and straightened up because my feet were already killing me in these spiked high heels that my roommate Shelly convinced me to buy that were two sizes too small because she said my feet looked like "freaking canoes." I already was working on a couple of blisters on top of the bunions that I already had from standing all day long at Beauty School cutting the hair of the cheapskate bimbos who came in for free haircuts.

"Are you Shelly Cramero?" asked the security guard, holding the phone.

"No, I'm Annabelle Stilletto," I said, trying to do the soft voice thing. "Shelly's my roommate. I'm here instead of her."

The guy looked at me like I was nuts or something, so I figured I better do something quick. I kind of leaned over and stuck my chest out again – which was really tough with the spiked heels and all – and then sort of whispered "Shelly said it was cool."

The guy stared at my boobs for a minute, and then nodded. "Okay, here's a visitor pass." He handed me a badge and watched closely as I pinned it to my blouse. The elevator's over there. Go to the third floor and ask for Mr. Griso."

I started off toward the elevators, stumbling slightly in my spiked heels. Then I stopped and turned back. "Senior or Junior?"

"Junior," replied the guard.

When the elevator door opened I couldn't believe my freaking eyes. There was this gorgeous blonde chick sitting behind a humongous desk – and this was only reception!

"Can I help you dear?" she said.

She was chewing gum which I think is kind of classless, but her makeup was really good and her hair was kind of Amy Winehouse but not in a bad way.

"Yeah," I said, teetering on my spiked heels. "I'm here to see Mr. Griso."

"Junior or Senior? " she asked, gazing at her nails, which I have to say were perfectly manicured and very pink, which is cool.

"Junior," I said.

With that, she gave me a look up and down, checking me out like I was some beauty contestant or something.

"Have a seat" she said finally. "I'll be right with you." So she got up and started for the door. She was wearing this really short tube skirt that I'd seen on sale at Forever 21 and wanted to buy it but Shelly told me my butt was too fat to wear anything like that. Suddenly I wished I'd bought it even though my butt is fat.

"Would you like a Coke or somethin'?" said the blonde as she chewed her gum.

"No, thanks," I said, and gave her a smile.

This was a classy place. It's not everywhere they give you free Cokes just for coming in for an interview. I figured it was much classier to say no, even though a diet Coke would hit the spot right now.

So I flip through a couple of magazines like People and US Weekly to catch up on what the movie stars are doing. I can't believe the way those people get divorced and treat each other bad. I mean, you can understand when people like my mom and Aunt Dolores get divorced because their husbands are nothing but lazy bums who've got nothing to offer. But you've got to be crazy to divorce Brad Pitt or even Charlie Sheen. Shit, maybe they do run around and screw other women but when you've got a humongous mansion in Beverly Hills and no limit on your credit cards and paparazzi camped out on the front lawn, what the hell to you have to complain about? Give me a friggin' break.

After a few minutes, the blonde comes out again. She gives me this funny look like "you don't know what you're in for" and says, "Mr. Griso will see you now."

I get up, trying to keep my balance on my spiked heels. "Come with me please," she says and heads through the door. I follow after her, kind of tiptoeing on the heels. And I suddenly get very nervous. I don't know what to expect. Is this guy going to be some old creep? She did say Mr. Griso Junior, didn't she? Still, the guy could be forty-two or something weird like that. What am I supposed to say to a forty-two year old guy?

So I'm heading down this long hallway toward the open door of a big office when I hear this voice from inside the office.

"Get me a cup of coffee, will you Teresa?"

I almost stopped dead in my spiked heels. His voice was so silky smooth like some kind of pop singer or something. It was like his voice floated out of the office and hit me right in the heart. I could almost hear rap music in my brain and I started to sway and my knees got weak. Get a hold of yourself, Annabelle, I told myself. He's probably some creepy guy who's working in his dad's business and wears glasses and a green visor or something.

As I turned the corner into the office, I started to look in the direction of the voice when I tripped on the rug, lost my balance, slipped off my heels and feel flat on my friggin' face. I'm not kidding, I was sprawled out on the rug, with my legs splayed in three directions, my hair messed up and my lipstick smudged. Then, all of a sudden,

I hear that voice again.

"Are you okay?"

I look up and there he is. The most gorgeous guy I've ever seen in my whole entire life. He couldn't have been more than thirty and had jet black hair, which was combed back and slick with gel. His eyes were clear blue and he was dressed in this shiny black outfit – shirt open halfway down his chest and tight pants with these like pointy black shoes. I could hardly look at him. Or even talk.

"Are you okay?" he asked again.

"Yeah, I'm fine," I mumbled.

"Let me help you up," he said. I couldn't believe it. Most of the guys I knew would just laugh at you and point if you fell off your heels. This guy was a real gentleman.

As he helped me get up, he got a glimpse of my thong under my skirt, which normally would have got me real embarrassed, but since he was so frigging cute, I figured that a free look was okay. Anyways, I couldn't really help it since I had to get my legs untangled before I could even manage standing up on the heels again. As I got up, I noticed that he was seriously checking me out, which was especially cool since that meant he wasn't gay or anything. But at the same time, he wasn't like staring or making gross remarks like the dumb punks that hang out around the corner from me. After I struggled to my feet, still teetering on my heels, he took my hand like a real gentleman, led me over to a couch and said gently,

"Would you like to sit down?"

"Sure," I said, plopping down onto the couch.

It was then I had a chance to really look around at the office. It was pretty impressive. It was real modern, with white rugs and white furniture. All white. There was this couch that looks Italian or something made of white leather and covered with clear plastic so it wouldn't get dirty. And there was a couple of chairs that were all white and looked kind of like BARCO Loungers, you know, the ones that you can recline all the way back in. Plus there was like original art from that famous artist DeRoy Neuman or whatever that was actually signed, although you couldn't actually read his signature because it was kind of messy.

Plus he had an actual bar in his office which was entirely stainless steel with a microwave and everything. And a whole bunch of wine bottles on like a rack that went all the way up to the ceiling and was enclosed in a glass case. I never saw anything like that before. Oh yeah, and he had a sound system which was unbelievable right in his office that could pound out the music incredibly loud but the whole office was soundproof so nobody else could hear, which I didn't find out until later, but that's a totally other story.

Anyways, so there I am sprawled out on this gorgeous guy's couch trying to recover from falling flat on my face and I'm starting to hyperventilate just looking at how hot he is.

That's when he says to me "You're not Shelly, are

you?"

Shit. And double shit. What am I supposed to say?

So I straighten out my skirt and stick out my chest
a little and say "No. I'm Annabelle. Annabelle Stilletto."
I'm really nervous because I'm afraid he's going to throw me
out of his office or something but instead he reaches out his
hand and says "Nice to meet you, Annabelle."

Can you believe it? Not only is this guy hot and a
gentleman, he's actually a really nice guy. I can't friggin' believe my luck. Here I am in a job interview with this dream
guy and he's actually being nice to me, even though my hair
is totally lame and I fell flat on my face right on his beautiful white rug. But then I had this moment of total panic
– what if he decides not to hire me? Then I'll be stuck back
in my lousy apartment with my stupid roommate Shelly and
her doofus boyfriend sitting on the couch watching pornos.
Right then, I decided I'd do anything to get this job. And I
mean anything!

"Nice to meet you, too, Mr. Griso," I say, real soft and
sweet.

"Call me Vinnie," he says, also soft and sweet. OMG!
He wants me to call him Vinnie. This is unreal. I can't wait
to text my mom and Aunt Dolores and even Shelly and
tell them I met this incredibly hot guy and he wants me to
call him "Vinnie." But I took a couple of deep breaths so
I wouldn't hyperventilate and just looked at up at him and
smiled and said. "Hi, Vinnie." And he smiled back! I felt I

was going to faint.

"So Annabelle...?" he said.

"Yes, Vinnie?" I answered him right away. I just wanted to say his name. A lot.

"You're looking for a job?"

"Yes, Vinnie. I am."

"What kind of job are you looking for?"

"Anything" As soon as I got the words out of my mouth, I wanted to take them back. I didn't want to sound that desperate, even though I was.

"Anything?" asked Vinnie. He was looking at me real intently and I almost hyperventilated again.

"That didn't sound right, did it?"

"Why not?" he said. I thought I could see a trace of a smile on those gorgeous lips.

I started to giggle and then he smiled and I felt better.

"Okay, let's start again," he said. "What kind of experience have you had?"

"Well, I've had three months of Beauty School and I've got a certificate in Hair Styling."

"Very impressive," he said. I couldn't tell if he was teasing me or something. But then I realized he was actually serious. This was incredible. How many guys would say shit like that and actually mean it? It was like I had been transported into an alternate universe or something.

"It was nothing," I said, trying to be modest. I even

tried to blush, but I can never pull that off.

"Are you kidding?" he replied. "This world needs more people like you who are attentive to personal appearance. Grooming is very important to me."

"It is?"

"Oh, yes. I take great care in maintaining my personal appearance. In fact, I pay attention to every detail of my life. I'm a big fan of discipline."

"Discipline?" I gasped.

"Definitely," he said. "No pain, no gain. That's my motto."

"You know, you're absolutely right."

This guy was truly incredible. Not like all the other lazy guys I'd met. Here was somebody who had a lot of confidence and really took care of himself. Plus he knew exactly how to treat women.

"So how would you like to work for me?"

I couldn't believe my ears. Was he really offering me a job? This was like a friggin' dream. After waking up with bad hair, getting hassled by the punks on the corner and falling flat on my face, this gorgeous guy wanted me to work for him? I could hardly speak.

"Uh...uh...uh. Yeah, I would."

"Good."

"When can you start?"

"Uh....right away."

"How about Monday?"

"That would be great..."

"Okay. But first we should probably work out some details."

"Sure. What kind of details?"

"Well, how much salary do you want?"

"Uh...I don't know."

"How about 75 grand to start?"

Holy shit. This guy was offering me 75 grand to work for him? That's like twice what even my friend Tiara was making and she's a friggin' secretary at an accounting firm in Manhattan.

"Uh...that's good."

"Good. Plus you'll probably need a new wardrobe."

Now I was really hyperventilating. Good thing I was sitting down.

"A new...?"

"Yeah. I'll have Sheila issue you a credit card. Go shopping. Buy whatever you want. We'll put it on my account."

I swear to God, I had just died and gone to heaven.

"....Okay."

"And how did you get here today?"

"I took the bus from Jersey City."

"That's no good. You're definitely going to need a car."

"But I can't afford..."

"Don't worry about it. We'll get a car for you."

"You will?"

"How about a Mustang? Red? Convertible?"

OMG. I can't breathe.

"That would be good."

"And where are you living now?"

"With my girlfriend Shelly. In an apartment in Jersey City."

"That won't do. We have a corporate condo right around the corner. It's fully furnished. Jacuzzi. Pool. Spa. The whole thing. Do you think you could move in there?"

Hold on a second, I thought. It suddenly dawned on me that Vinnie might have something else in mind besides a job. I'd read about these rich guys who set up their mistresses in apartments and bought them clothes and cars while they cheated on their wives. That didn't sound terrible, of course. But at least I wanted to know what I was getting into. I glanced down at his left hand ring finger.

"You're not married, are you?"

"Nope."

"Separated?"

"Nope."

"Divorced?"

"Never married. Why do you ask?"

I didn't know how to answer. But I figured I should try. I wanted to get things straight before I got into a situation I didn't know how to get out of. All the clothes and car and apartment and everything sounded great, but exactly what did this guy expect?

"Well, I was just wondering exactly what kind of work you wanted me to do."

"I want you to be my personal assistant."

"What does that mean exactly?"

"It means that you will take care of my person – everything that I need and want."

"Everything?"

"Everything."

I thought about that for a minute.

"I'm still confused about what you want me to do."

Vinnie looked at me and smiled.

"Don't worry. I'll spell everything out for you in the contract."

"The contract?"

"Yep. I'll send you a contract to sign that has all the rules laid out exactly."

"The rules?"

"Yeah. I like to operate with a certain set of rules for all my employees."

"Oh."

"Are you okay with rules?"

"Oh, yeah. I like rules. I think."

"Good. But if you have any problems with any of the rules, you can tell me and we can discuss them. Is that okay?"

"Sure."

"The main thing is that you agree with the rules. Because I want you to be completely satisfied. Okay?"

There was something about the way he said "completely satisfied" that made me a little wobbly in the knees. I'm not sure if it was the spiked heels or what, but I was definitely feeling some amazing vibes from this guy.

"Yeah, great," I said.

"Cool. Because I'm all about rules. You know, discipline."

"Oh, yeah," I said. "Rules. Discipline. I know what you mean."

Actually, I wasn't really sure what he was talking about. All I could think about was his blue eyes and his jet black hair and also what kind of clothes I was going to buy to go with my new red Mustang convertible and my fully furnished condo.

"Great. So I'll draw up the contract and have it sent over to you. Then maybe we can meet for a drink and discuss it. If you have any questions about the rules, we can talk about it then. Okay?"

"Yeah. Terrific. Thank you so much, Vinnie."

"No, thank you, Annabelle."

I didn't know what else to say, so I started to back out of the office.

"See you soon," he said briskly, giving me a little wave.

"See you soon," I said, kind of breathlessly, and I

wasn't even faking it. I was seriously hyperventilating just looking at this guy. My legs were like jelly and I was afraid I was going to trip again but I made it out the door okay. I kind of leaned against the wall to catch my breath when the blonde secretary comes over to me.

"Are you alright?"

"I'm fine," I said, but she knew I wasn't really. She gave me this kind of knowing smile like "He's really hot, isn't he?" But she didn't have to say anything because I knew what she was thinking.

I rushed out of the building and right away pulled out my iPhone. I couldn't wait to start texting. I didn't know who to text first – Shelly, or my mother, or my Aunt Dolores. So I texted Shelly.

"OMG Shel u wont believe it. This guy is so HOTTTTTTT!!"

"What guy????"

"The frggnnn interview!!"

"OMG"

"I got the job + he's buying me clothes & car."

"WTF!!!!!"

"ohyeah"

Right then the bus came so I had to get on, but all the way home I was texting everybody I knew, including my mom and Aunt Dolores who thought it was kind of weird even though they were happy. I told them it was cool and that he was going to send me this contract and everything with rules, so what could be bad? I was so excited I knew I wasn't going to sleep for like a week. Every time I closed my eyes, I knew I'd be thinking about his gorgeous black hair and his shiny tight pants and pointy shoes and his clear blue eyes. And that voice. So soft and sweet. Swear to God, I've died and gone to heaven.

Chapter Two

So later that night, while Shelly's doofus boyfriend was watching pornos on the couch, me and Shelly go outside for a smoke on the stoop. I'm so friggin' excited to tell her about Mr. Hot Guy Vinnie but I don't want her stupid boyfriend to hear about any of it. I wasn't sure if Shelly was going to be jealous or anything but I was bursting to tell her everything.

"Omygod, Shel, you wouldn't believe how gorgeous he is..."

"Really?"

"Abso-fucking-lutely."

"So tell," she said, lighting up a Virginia Slim.

"Okay, so he's tall..."

"How tall?"

"I dunno. Six feet maybe..."

"What? Six feet two?"

"No, not that tall."

"Five-ten?"

"No, taller than that. But will you let me finish already?"

"Sure," she said, taking a long drag on her Virginia Slim.

"Okay, so he's tall and has this gorgeous black hair."

"Gelled?"

"A little gelled maybe."

"How about his eyes?"

"I'm getting to his eyes, okay?"

"Excuse me for living," said Shelly, taking another puff.

"His eyes....are totally blue. Like clear blue."

"Like the sky?"

"No, not like the sky."

"Like dark blue?"

"No. Light blue. Like the ocean."

"That's cool."

"No shit."

"What was he wearing?"

"Okay, that's the best part. He was wearing...all black!"

"All black?"

"Totally black."

"That's hot."

"No shit. Black pants."

"Tight?"

"Totally tight."

"Ouch."

"And...a tight shirt."

"Unbuttoned...?"

"Yep, halfway down his chest."

"Omygod. What about his chest?"

"Totally buff."

"How about his shoes?"

"Black. Pointy."

"I'm dying over here."

"I couldn't hardly talk to him..."

"I shoulda gone to that interview instead of you."

"You didn't want to go..."

"I know. And now I'm stuck with my stupid boy-friend and you've got Mr. Hot and Buff."

"And rich."

"Is he really going to pay you 75 grand?"

"That's what he said."

"Plus buy you a car and a condo?"

"Yep."

"So what's the catch?"

"I don't know."

"There must be a catch."

"I guess."

"Is he married?"

"No."

"Separated?"

"Nope. "

"Divorced?"

"Never married."

"Holy shit, Annabelle."

"Yeah. It's like I won the fucking lottery."

"You go, girl."

With that, me and Shelly traded high fives and did a quick chest bump. She took another puff on her Virginia Slims and then kind of leaned over and said in a low voice.

"So are you like his mistress or what?"

I looked at her, totally shocked.

"What do mean?"

"I mean the guy is paying you 75 grand and buying you a car and a condo. He must be expecting something."

"He wants me to be his personal assistant."

"Oh, yeah. Personal, I bet," she said, rolling her eyes.

"What are you talking about, Shelly?" I asked. She was starting to piss me off.

"Come off it, Annabelle, the guy wants to jump your bones. What's wrong with that?"

"You really think so?"

"Sure, why the hell else would he be buying you all that shit?"

I didn't know whether I was supposed to be insulted or flattered. Actually, it was a bit of both. Maybe Vinnie was disrespecting me, but it also got me a little excited that he was so hot for my bod that he was shelling out the big bucks. Who knew I was worth that kind of money? Not that I don't have self-esteem. I have plenty of self-esteem.

It's just that I never actually thought about how much money somebody would pay...Hold on, what the hell am I thinking?

"You know I'm not that kind of girl, Shel."

She rolled her eyes.

"No? Well, I sure as hell am."

I didn't know I wanted to continue this conversation. It wasn't exactly going in a terrific direction. Sure, it was cool that Vinnie was hot and everything. And I couldn't believe he was going to pay all that money for me to be his personal assistant. But on the other hand, did he think I was a slut or something?

"Besides, Shel, I'm not that experienced, you know."

"Bullshit."

"I'm not. I've barely had sex before."

"That is such bullshit, Annabelle. What about Tony de Marco?"

"Yeah, big deal. Three times in the back of his Honda."

"You told me it was fantastic."

"I lied, okay. He came in about three seconds and then he bragged about it to all his stupid friends."

"Okay. Then how about Phil Redman? "

"What about him?"

"You had sex with him."

"I did not."

"You gave him a blow job."

"That doesn't count. And it was only that one time in the alley behind the Yard House. Plus I was drunk."

"Still. And how about Bobby Tarkenian?"

"A hand job. Maybe two. Does that make me a slut?"

"I didn't say you were a slut."

"You implied it."

"All I said was that this Vinnie guy is not paying you all that money just for the pleasure of your company."

Now I was getting really angry. Here was Shelly who spends all day long sitting on her fat ass and all she wants to do is criticize me and call me a slut.

"How do you know, Shelly?" I said, standing up. "How do you know that? Maybe he thinks I'm cute. Did you ever think of that? Maybe he's attracted to me. Or is that so impossible for you to believe?"

"Listen, Annabelle, I'm sorry..."

"Go to hell!"

I was really pissed and started to go back inside the apartment. Just then, my cell phone rang. I looked down at the number but didn't recognize it.

"Hello?"

"Is this Miss Stilletto?"

It was a voice I didn't recognize. Kind of low and raspy.

"Yes, this is Annabelle."

"My name is T-Bomb."

That was a scary name. I was almost going to hang up but I was suddenly pretty curious what this was about.

"Do I know you?"

"I work for Mr. Griso."

My heart started to flutter, along with my knees, my hands and a bunch of other places.

"Junior or Senior?" I asked.

"Junior," he answered.

"Oh..." Now I was really getting excited.

"Mr. Griso would like you to join him for dinner."

OMG. Vinnie was asking me out for dinner! Well, not Vinnie exactly – his employee, T-Bomb.

"Uh...sure," I said, not wanting to sound too eager. "When?"

"Now. I'm around the corner in the limo. I'll pick you up in five minutes."

Holy shit! I was going out to dinner with Vinnie Griso! What the hell was I going to wear? And how the fuck was I supposed to get dressed in five minutes??

"Wait a sec..." I said into the phone, but T-Bomb had already hung up. "Hello??"

Oh, shit. What am I going to do? I turned around and went back to Shelly, who was still puffing on her Virginia Slim.

"Shelly, you gotta help me."

I was starting to hyperventilate.

"What's wrong?"

"I need your help.."

I grabbed her hand and yanked her up the stoop.

"Who was that on the phone?"

"T-Bomb," I muttered.

"Who the hell is T-Bomb?"

"I'll explain later," I said, rushing into the apartment. Shelly ran in after me.

"What's going on?"

"I've got to get dressed right now."

"Why?"

"Because I'm going out to dinner with Vinnie."

"The Vinnie?"

"Yes!"

"Holy shit!"

"That was his driver. He's right around the corner and he's picking me up in a limo in five minutes and taking me to dinner."

"What are you going to wear?"

"I don't know!!"

So Shelly and I rushed into my bedroom and started flinging clothes onto the bed.

"Pick out something sexy while I put on my make-up!" I shouted from the bathroom.

"How sexy?"

"Very sexy!"

Next thing you know I was pulling on a really tight low-cut blouse and short vinyl skirt. I checked my butt out in the mirror.

"Does this make me look fat?"

"No way," said Shelly.

I turned and stared at her.

"Shel, this is really important. You can't lie to me. Does this make me look fat?"

She stared at me for a moment, then said quietly.

"Yes..."

"Omygod!"

I felt like I was gonna cry. Here I was getting ready for the most important dinner of my life and I was fat. I had to get a hold of myself.

"Okay," I said, my lower lip quivering. "Which part?"

"Your butt," said Shelly.

"I knew it. My butt is fat!"

"It's not that fat."

"It's huge. It's humongous!" I said, bursting into tears.

"It's not humongous," said Shelly, trying to comfort me.

"It's just a little wide."

"My butt is wide!??" I shrieked.

"Calm down, Annabelle. We can fix it."

"How can we fix my butt in five minutes??"

I was definitely hyperventilating now.

"Here, all you have to do is tuck your blouse out."

She reached over and pulled my blouse over my skirt. I looked up and down at myself in the mirror.

"Are you sure?"

"Positive."

"I don't look fat?"

"No. Plus you've got great tits. He'll be looking at them and not your butt."

"Do I really have great tits?"

"Abso-fucking-lutely. I wish I had your tits."

"Really?"

"Promise."

"You're the best, Shel."

I gave her a big hug. Just then the doorbell rang.

"Oh, shit. He's here."

"Don't worry. You'll do fine."

"Thanks, Shel."

I gave myself one more look in the mirror, took a deep breath and went to the door. When I opened it I saw this really tall guy dressed in a black suit and shades with one of those earpieces like the celebrity bodyguards have.

"Miss Stilletto?"

"Yes?"

"My name is T-Bomb."

"Nice to meet you, Mr. Bomb."

"My pleasure."

"Are you ready to go?"

I wasn't sure whether that was an insult or something. Or maybe I was just being insecure. Didn't I look ready? Was he saying there was something wrong with me? Sometimes when I get nervous, I start chewing on the inside of my check. It's a bad habit I know, but when I'm nervous I kind of fall into it. I know it's weird and all, but I can't help it. Anyway, I decided the guy wasn't insulting me, or at least he wasn't doing it intentionally. So I just smiled.

"Yeah, I'm ready."

"Come with me, Miss Stilletto."

I gulped and followed him out the door, casting a quick glance back at Shelly, who gave me the thumbs up sign.

I was so nervous as I followed T-Bomb down the steps of my stoop that I thought I might fall flat on my face. Plus I was worried that the stupid punks from the corner would see me and yell out something about my fat ass. But luckily, they weren't anywhere around.

When I got to the bottom of the steps I almost fainted. There was the biggest friggin' white stretch limo that I'd ever seen in my life. OMG Annabelle Stilletto, what have you gotten yourself into?

T-Bomb opened the door to the limo and helped me climb inside. I didn't know what to expect, but what I saw completely blew me away. The whole interior of the limo was covered in white leather. White leather rugs, white leather seats, white leather bar, white leather whips....wait a second? What is with the whips?

I told myself it was probably okay. Maybe Vinnie goes riding and needs them for his polo horses. Or else he's an elephant trainer or something as a hobby. Still, it gave me a kind of queasy feeling seeing the whips, so I tried not stare at them or anything.

"Would you like a glass of champagne, Miss Stilletto?" asked T-Bomb from the front seat.

"Uh, sure..." I said. If nothing else, it would calm my nerves.

He pushed a button on the dashboard of the limo and suddenly a little trap door opened next to my seat and a glass of bubbly champagne in a beautiful crystal glass emerged, almost like magic.

"What the hell...?"

T-Bomb smiled.

"Just one of the many special features of Mr. Griso's ride."

I took a gulp of champagne. It was delicious and tingled my nose. I was already tingling from head to toe, so the alcohol just added to my excitement.

"So...where is Vin...er...Mr. Griso?" I asked sweetly.

"You'll see," he answered mysteriously.

With that, T-Bomb cranked up the sound system and whole limo started shaking with Snoop Dog. I leaned back and took another sip of the bubbly champagne. I felt like Cinderella, riding in her carriage, wondering what was going to happen next. Was the limo going to suddenly turn into a pumpkin and I would wake up from this incredible dream?

Chapter Three

I was already feeling a little tipsy when the limo pulled onto the Palisades Parkway. I could see the bright lights of Manhattan in the distance and the George Washington Bridge stretched out like Christmas tree lights across the Hudson River. Since I don't have a car, I don't get to see the view from the Palisades very often. It's got to be the most romantic view anywhere in Jersey.

And I was in a pretty romantic mood, or maybe it was the champagne. All I could think about was Vinnie Griso, standing there in his tight black pants and his blue eyes and pointy shoes. I understood what Shelly was trying to tell me – that he wasn't going to pay me 75 grand and give me a new wardrobe and a car and a condo just to be his personal assistant.

Okay, he probably had something else in mind. But even if he did, it didn't have to be anything gross and disgusting. Maybe he was just attracted to me. Is that so impossible? That a really hot guy would be attracted to me? After all, I'm pretty hot if I do say so myself, even if my butt is fat.

Even Shelly said I had great tits, which is saying a lot.

Maybe it's one of those things you read about books or see in the movies where it's like love at first sight. You know, where the guy looks across a crowded room and sees this beautiful woman and their eyes meet and he falls instantly in love but is too shy to talk to her until she sort of flutters her eyes in his direction and he gets up the guts to go over and ask her to dance and the next thing you know they are drinking wine and talking all night and then they get engaged and get married and have a honeymoon in Atlantic City and get a detached house in Teaneck and have two point five children.

I guess was getting a little tipsy because the next thing I knew we were exiting the Parkway in Alpine. OMG. Friggin' Alpine!! That's where all these amazing celebrities live like Snooki and Howard Stern and J-Lo. I was going to text Shelly right away but then I thought maybe she'd be jealous or else she'd get scared that I was going to be kidnapped by the Mafia since there most of The Sopranos was filmed in Alpine and the actual Tony Soprano had a house there.

Anyways, I looked out the window at all the mansions going by and couldn't friggin' believe it. I mean, I've seen mansions before on TV shows like Pimp My Crib and The Kardashians but these places were even more incredible. You couldn't even see the friggin' houses from the road. They were surrounded by huge walls and gates that had somebody's initials on them. They probably had guard dogs and machine guns and radar or something to keep the paparazzi and the groupies away.

So we finally pull into this long driveway that has a humongous iron gate with like these fierce-looking lions decorating it. And also these weird faces that look like something on those big churches I'd seen in Newark. What do they call them? Gargoons or gargoyles or something. They look more like vampires to me. The undead. I got a chill looking up at the lions and vampires as the gates slowly opened up.

"Where are we, T-Bomb?" I asked. I admit I was a little nervous.

"Mr. Griso's house," he said quietly.

I looked down the long driveway. At the end of it was this house that looked like a cross between the White House and the Jersey City Mall. I swear it was the biggest house I'd ever seen, even on TV. It was lit up with floodlights and everything and looked like some kind of palace from England or somewhere. No wonder I felt like Cinderella. All I needed now was a prince. And I was hoping it would be Mr. Vinnie Griso, the prince of auto parts.

As we got nearer the Griso palace, I was even more astounded at how big it was. They always say size doesn't matter – at least that's what Shelly always says – but when it comes to houses, bigger is definitely better. And this place was definitely better. To begin with, it was all white, which made it dazzle in the floodlights. It had these enormous white columns that looked like pure marble in the front, and there were these statues of Greek gods or whatever – all totally nude. Plus all the statues were all holding weapons in their hands – like whips and chains and stuff which I thought was pretty cool, although maybe it should have given me a hint about Vinnie Griso's tastes, but I'll get to that later.

On every corner of the roof there were these huge towers that you read about in fairy tales. I half expected Rapunzel or some blonde chick with long hair to wave at me from one of the towers. Or maybe Spiderman would swing down from one of the towers and hop on the roof of the limo. Also there were lots more gargoons or vampires or whatever the heck they were. This place was definitely classy. All the towers were dark inside, except one tower – the tallest one of them all –which had a very faint light coming through the window. That must be where he keeps the girls he captures and ravishes, I thought to myself.

But then I quickly put all that out of my mind. After all, this was Vinnie Griso, Mr. Rich Hottie, the guy I had met that very morning and treated me like a true gentleman. Maybe Shelly thought there might be something weird about him, but I knew he was a perfectly nice guy. I couldn't wait to go inside the mansion and see what Mr. Griso had in store for me that evening.

I was trembling with excitement as the limo pulled up in front of the mansion. I quickly checked myself out in my hand mirror, touching my lipstick and mascara. I had picked out the darkest shade of lipstick I could find – basic black – since I thought maybe that would be a special turn-on for

Vinnie. I don't know why, but I had this feeling that he was definitely into black. So I hit the black mascara pretty heavy too, and added a little Amy Winehouse fake mole to go with my teased hair and, of course, my trademark stilettos. They don't call me Annabelle Stilletto for nothing.

So when T-Bomb opened the door to the limo, I was definitely ready to make a big entrance. Normally I would have been hyperventilating if you told me I was going to meet this incredible Prince Charming who was rich and handsome and a real gentleman. But somehow I felt real calm, like this was meant to be. This was going to be my big romantic moment – like meeting across a crowded room – where Vinnie and I had fallen in love at first sight, and this was going to be the beginning of my own real life fairy tale.

That's when I fell down. Hard. I mean WHAM! right on my friggin' rear end.

"Shit!!" I yelled out real loud. I couldn't help it. It hurt like hell.

"Fuck!!" I yelled, even louder as T-Bomb rushed over to help me.

I felt like a total idiot but also I was hurting and when I saw blood starting to ooze from my elbow, I couldn't help myself – I started to cry.

"I can believe this is happening!" I wailed.

"It's okay, it's okay..." T-Bomb kept repeating, but he didn't know what to do.

"It's not okay!!" I moaned.

Just then, none other than Vinnie Griso came rushing out of the house. He was dressed in tuxedo and even through my tears I couldn't help noticing how gorgeous he looked.

He rushed over and kneeled down next to me.

"Are you okay?" he said, his voice dripping with tenderness and concern.

"Noooo!!"

"What happened?" he asked, trying to calm me down.

"I fell down!" I cried.

He took my right ankle gently in his hand and pressed it softly.

"Does this hurt?"

"No," I murmured.

"How about this?" he asked, testing the other ankle.

"No."

"Good. Let me take a look at your elbow."

"Alright," I said, sniffling. Despite the pain, I was starting to feel a lot better. Something about Vinnie's soft voice and gentle touch that calmed me down.

"Are you a doctor or something?" I asked, only half-joking.

"No, but I was a medic in Iraq. I've treated a lot of wounds."

Wow. This guy had done everything. Taking care of wounded soldiers. What a brave guy. In fact, he probably single-handedly saved America from all those crazy terrorists. Or not. I had to get a hold of myself.

"That elbow looks pretty raw. Let's get you into the house and clean it up."

"Okay," I said meekly, looking up into those clear blue eyes.

Together Vinnie and T-Bomb hoisted me to my feet and helped me into the house. The whole time I was thinking how cool it was to be encircled with Vinnie's strong arms, to rest my head on his neck and to smell his Brut cologne. At the same time, I hoped he wasn't looking too closely at my ass, which I had decided was still way too fat, no matter what Shelly said.

They carried me though the door into what looked like a huge living room but I later found out was what they called the "entryway." I swear to God it must have been three stories high with this humongous chandelier that looked like it was made out of diamonds and would kill you if it ever fell on you. Plus there was this gorgeous wall-to-wall carpeting everywhere. Did I mention that Vinnie loves white décor? White furniture. White carpets. White beds. Except for his clothes, which are always black, which I think is so cool.

Anyways, they lay me down on this great big white sectional leather couch and I'm staring at the ceiling which is painted in this Italian style like the Sistine Chapel or something. Of course, I've never been to Rome or anything, but I've seen the pictures. OMG this ceiling looked like it was painted by Michael Angelo. It was truly amazing with angels and cupids and everything. I don't know if Jesus was in there, but he should have been, it was so beautiful. So I almost forgot about how my elbow was bleeding until Vinnie took this silk handkerchief out of his pocket and started very gently dabbing at my bloody elbow.

"Does that hurt?" he asked in this real low and sexy voice.

"Not really."

I smiled up at him and looked into his clear blue eyes. Honestly, you could've stuck an ice pick in my neck right then and I wouldn't have felt anything. All I could see was those big blue eyes and the soft touch of his hand on my arm.

"Are you sure you want to get that handkerchief all bloody?" I asked.

"Oh, it's nothing," he said.

"It looks like it's silk."

"It is. From Ceylon."

"Wow. It must've been pretty expensive."

"Not really. Three hundred maybe."

"Three hundred dollars?"

"Around that."

OhmyGod, he spent three hundred dollars for a silk handkerchief and now here he was ruining it just for me. Heck, I would've been happy with a piece of gauze.

Just then I looked up at him. I knew I shouldn't say anything but I just couldn't help myself.

"You're very sweet."

"Not really," he said. There was something in the way he said it that was sort of peculiar.

"No, you really are. I can't believe how sweet you are."

He gave a kind of a half-smile.

"Maybe after you get to know me better, you won't feel the same way."

"I'll always feel the same way," I said. I knew I shouldn't have said that. It was going too far. But I couldn't help myself. I was getting swept away by this guy. I had never felt this way about anyone before. He was so sweet and kind and gentle and definitely hot.

Right then, I knew I had to get a hold of myself. I could hear Shelly's voice telling me not to get too carried away. "Guys can sense that," she would say, "And then they take advantage of you." I knew she was right, but there was something about Vinnie Griso that made me want him to take advantage of me. Right here, right now.

Chapter Four

After Vinnie had bandaged up my elbow and I'd recovered a bit – at least from falling flat on my face – if not from swooning over Vinnie as he tenderly dressed my wound, he led me into the dining room. Actually, it wasn't the formal dining room – this guy has a formal dining room and an "informal" dining room – that's how rich he is. The formal dining room looks like fifty people could have dinner in there, including the Queen of England and fucking Angelina Jolie. It had to be as big as a barn with this huge table made out of some kind of fancy carved wood.

Anyways, Vinnie took me into the "informal" dining room, which was about the size of my entire apartment, and was filled with floor-to-floor ceiling bookshelves that were stocked with fake books that opened up and had stuff like vodka and tequila in them, or else fancy cigars. One even opened up and had chocolate chip cookies and Doritos, which are absolutely my favorite but I try to stay away from them since, as I might have mentioned, my ass is too fat.

In the middle of the room was this table with a

white table cloth and a single rose in a gorgeous crystal vase. There were two place settings with amazing china and silverware and these serving dishes that looked like they were made from 100% sterling silver. And standing next to the table was this butler dressed in a tuxedo and holding a bottle of wine in one hand and a white napkin draped over his arm – like you see in the movies. Vinnie led me over to the table and pulled out my chair like a real gentlemen while the butler kind of bowed and poured me a glass of wine.

"Annabelle, this is Stewart, my butler."

"Good evening, Miss Stilletto."

OMG even the butler knew my name!

"Good evening, Stewart."

I tried to sound cool and sophisticated, but even so I was starting to hyperventilate again, so I took a sip of wine to keep from passing out.

"How do you like the wine, Annabelle?" asked Vinnie.

"Really good," I said. "Except I only ever had two buck Chuck before so what the hell do I know."

Vinnie smiled. I could get lost in the smile.

"I hope you like Chicken Cordon Bleu," he said.

"I hope so, too." I replied. "What the heck is it?"

"It's chicken stuffed with cheese and ham."

"Chicken, cheese and ham – what could be bad?" I said, taking another gulp of wine. I was starting to get really nervous in this fancy house with the fancy butler and gorgeous Mr. Griso with all this crazy food and elegant china and expensive wine.

As you may already know, when I get nervous I start to hyperventilate, so I had another gulp of wine to calm down. But I also have this habit of chewing on the inside of my cheek, which is pretty annoying because it gets red and swollen and it also looks from the outside like I'm chewing on a big wad of gum and I look sort of like a chipmunk that has swallowed a nut.

Vinnie stared at me. I guess he noticed.

"Don't do that," he said sternly.

"Do what?" I asked, even though I knew exactly what he was talking about.

"That," he said, pointing to my cheek.

"Oh, this?" I said. I was trying to stop but I got so nervous that I started chewing my cheek twice as bad.

"Yes, that."

"I can't help it. I do it when I get nervous."

"Do I make you nervous?"

"Well....yes!"

"How come?"

"All this. Your house, your butler, your wine, your china, your silverware."

"My silverware makes you nervous?"

"Hell yes."

"Why?"

"Because it's so....nice!"

I could feel my lower lip start to quiver and I was afraid I was going to cry, but instead I got more nervous and started chewing the inside of my cheek again.

"Don't do that!" said Vinnie, even louder. I could see he was starting to get really upset.

"Why not?" I asked. "What's the big deal?"

He looked over and stared at me with those big blue eyes. Something in his look changed for only a second, as if I was suddenly looking into the depths of his soul. And finally, slowly, he answered me.

"Because it really turns me on."

OhmyGod. I can't believe it. I'm turning on Vinnie Griso, incredibly rich hottie. It was like I was hyperventilating to the max. And I was like tingling all over. I had never felt this way before. At least not since the first time I watched Jersey Shore.

"I don't know what to say..."

"Don't say anything. Just stop chewing your cheek, or I'm going to have to fuck you right here on this table."

Okay, that was too much. I suddenly had this vision of Vinnie Griso suddenly sweeping away all that expensive china and silverware and the fine wine and crystal and crashing it all to the floor while he ravished me right there on the table in front of the butler and everything. Vinnie wasn't the only one getting really turned on.

"Oh, gosh," I said. That may have been kind of a

stupid thing to say. But then what I said next sounded even more stupid. "Don't you at least want to have dinner?"

He looked at me and then burst out in a big fat grin.

"I don't know if I can wait," he said, smiling.

I didn't know what to say so I took another big huge gulp of wine. Help!

"It's okay. Stewart, please bring in the Chicken Cordon Bleu."

"Certainly, sir."

Frankly, I wasn't hungry at all. Except for a delicious dish named Vinnie Griso. I looked over at his eyes and his hair and his luscious mouth and I thought all I want to eat right now is Vinnie. Every single part of him. I had to practically hold myself down from jumping his bones. I think he had the same idea about me. This was pure bliss.

Somehow we managed to restrain ourselves while we ate this incredible meal. I had never had Chicken Whatchamacallit before but it was really tasty – sort of like a big Chicken McNugget but filled with ham and cheese. And we had asparagus with butter which I usually don't like but there was something about the asparagus sitting there on the plate with its tip dripping in butter that made me want to have sex with Vinnie immediately if not sooner.

Finally, we finished dinner and I guess we were both a little drunk so he had the butler Stewart light a fire in the fireplace and bring me a Pink Cosmo which is my absolute favorite drink while Vinnie had a brandy. We were sitting there kind of stretched out on this really nice white leather sofa in front of the fire and I was just waiting expectantly for him to kiss me. I was gazing into his eyes and kind of leaning over towards him so he could get a good look at my eyes. It was a magical moment and I thought he was just about to make a move when he leaned over towards me, and whispered in my ear, in this low, sexy voice.

"I want to show you something."

There was something about the way he said it that sent chills down my spine, but not exactly in a bad way. It was like he was opening up a secret window for me into his world. It sounded a little scary, but at this point, I was so crazy about this guy, I was up for practically anything.

Vinnie took my hand and led me over to the bookcase. He scanned the bookshelf for a moment and then pointed to a copy of The Story of O, which I never read but I heard was pretty hot. He pulled the book off of the shelf and all of a sudden the whole entire bookshelf swung open and behind it there was this doorway with a purple velvet rope hanging in front of it. I was pretty surprised and let out kind of a gasp and jumped back. But Vinnie took me by the waist and then guided my hand up to the velvet rope.

"Pull it," he said softly.

At this point, I was going to do anything he told me, even though it occurred to me that maybe it was some kind of trap door that would drop me into a pool of alligators or something. But I didn't care. I pulled on the rope. Nothing happened.

"Pull it harder," he whispered.

"Okay. I'll try."

I gave the rope a hard yank and suddenly the door disappeared into the floor. Inside the door was nothing but darkness.

"Go ahead," said Vinnie, guiding me into the darkness. But I hesitated.

"What's wrong?" he said. "Are you afraid?"

"Kind of," I mumbled. This was starting to get a little weird. And as much as I wanted to do exactly what Vinnie told me, I was beginning to get scared.

"There's nothing to be afraid of," he said. "Here, I'll lead the way."

He took my hand and right away I felt better. He led me into the darkness and I heard the door close behind me. OhmyGod, I thought, now I'm really trapped. I could die in here and nobody would know. I probably can't even get cell service inside this place. Still, I'd gone this far, there was no going back now.

We stood there in total darkness for a minute, then Vinnie whispered to me.

"You ready?"

By this time, my voice was shaking.

"For what?"

"You'll see..." he said mysteriously.

Then, very slowly, a dim light appeared off to one

side. I could still barely see anything, but the light began to grower brighter, almost like a candle flickering in the darkness. I squinted around and saw that this was a room about the same size as the dining room but very different. First off, there were all these contraptions around the room and on the walls. I couldn't see them too clearly, but one looked like a giant spinning wheel like out of Jeopardy or something, and then there was what seemed like a trapeze swinging overhead. And on one wall there were all these different kinds of swords and whips and crazy stuff. As I looked around I started to get a very funny feeling in the pit of my stomach.

"What is this place?"

Vinnie smiled.

"I call it Vinnie's Secret Hideaway."

"Kind of like a clubhouse?"

"More like a playroom."

"What kind of playroom?"

"A playroom for Vinnie and his special friends."

My heart sank. Even though I wasn't sure exactly what he did in here, I right away got jealous that he might be doing it with other women.

"What special friends?"

"My friends who turn me on."

I couldn't help myself, but when he said that I started to melt right there. What he was saying was that I, Annabelle Stilletto from Jersey City, New Jersey, Annabelle with the fat ass and no car and a roommate with a stupid boyfriend actually turned him on. None other than Vinnie Griso, incredibly rich hottie. Still, I didn't like the idea that he was doing this with a bunch of other women.

"And who are these friends?"

"Right now, there aren't any."

My heart leapt. Was it really true that I was the only one of his "special friends." True, I didn't know exactly what it meant to be one of Vinnie's "special friends," but I was pretty flattered. Here was this rich handsome guy. Surely he must have women falling all over him.

"You mean there's nobody else?"

"Nope."

"How can that be? "

" I am very selective, Annabelle."

Ohmygod, I can't believe what I am hearing. Of course, he's very selective. He could have any woman he wanted. And he chose me. Right then I wished I had cell phone service so I could text Shelly. Partly because I wanted her to hear the good news right away, and partly because I wanted to prove to her that having a fat ass did not stand in the way of true love. Or at least I hoped it would be true love.

I looked around Vinnie's Secret Hideaway again and my imagination went wild. Part of me was really scared and grossed out by the stuff I saw in there. But another part of me was sort of curious – even excited – by what I was looking at. I tried to imagine myself with Vinnie in there, but I couldn't quite picture it. What exactly did he do with all this stuff? Or actually, what exactly did he do to women with this stuff? I was really curious, and I knew I had to ask him.

"So I have a question, Vinnie."

"Fire away."

"What do exactly to you do in here?"

"I play"

"Yeah, but what does that mean?"

"I give pleasure. To myself and others."

I glanced around the room.

"I'm not sure I understand exactly. Does all this stuff give you pleasure?"

"It helps me give pleasure...and get pleasure."

Okay, that didn't explain it exactly. So I thought I'd try another angle.

"Actually, it looks like some of this stuff might really hurt."

"Depends on what you mean by 'hurt.'"

"You know, like pain. Ouch? Owiee?"

"It only hurts if you want it to hurt. But it can also give you pleasure. A lot of pleasure."

"How?"

"I can show you if you want me to."

I looked over at him, into those clear blue eyes. While part of me wanted to run screaming out of the room and back to my apartment in Jersey City with Shelly, there was another part of me that really wanted to find out what he was talking about. I especially wanted to find out all about Vinnie Griso. I wanted to know every inch of him, inside and out.

"Maybe." I said.

"When?" he shot back.

Suddenly, I saw a look in his eyes. It wasn't quite desperate, but I could tell he wanted me bad. My knees went all shaky and I almost fell into his arms right then, but instead I got really nervous and started biting the inside of my cheek.

"Don't do that," he said.

"What?" I replied. I didn't even realize I what I was doing.

"That," he said pointing to my cheek. "It really turns me on and I can't stand it."

Wow. I was starting to get pretty hot myself. I figured it would be a good idea to change the subject, but I didn't know where to start.

"Nice whips," I said, pretending to admire one of the leather whips on the wall that looked about ten feet long. As soon as I said it, I realized that was probably the wrong thing to say. Plus it wasn't exactly changing the subject.

"Thanks," said Vinnie with a grin. "I had them made specially."

At this point I figured I'm in Vinnie's Secret Hide-way full of whips and chains and God knows what with this rich cute guy whose obviously got some pretty strange tastes. What's the point in beating around the bush? So I asked.

"So are you like a sadist or something?"

He chuckled.

"No, I'm a 'top.'"

"What's that?"

"You've heard of the Alpha Male?"

"Yeah, like Donald Trump?"

"Exactly. I'm like Donald Trump."

That actually sounded okay to me.

"So you order people around and fire them?"

"Sort of. I order people around but I don't fire them very often. Unless they disobey me."

"But you still make them to do things with all these whips and chains and stuff?"

"Not unless they want to."

"I don't get it. Why would anybody want to have you do things to them with whips and chains?"

"Because they want to please me."

Ooookay. I was starting to get the picture. This was all about pleasing Mr. Vinnie Griso. That was the whole personal assistant deal he told me about at his office. Actually, part of me really wanted to please Vinnie. In fact, there were lots of parts of me that wanted to please him right here, right now. But then there was a small part of me that was wondering "What the hell are you getting yourself into, Annabelle Stilletto?" I could end up really busted up and bruised or even worse.

"And if they don't want to please you?"

Vinnie's face grew dark for a moment, then he smiled.

"Then we end the arrangement. No hard feelings. I never force anyone to do anything. That's why I have the Rules."

"The Rules?"

"Yep. Do you want to see them?"

Uh-oh. I've never been big on rules. At Catholic school, the nuns always had a bunch of bullshit rules and I was always breaking them because half the time I never remembered what the rules were in the first place or else I forgot about them right away. The fact is, I want to do what I want to do and I don't like anybody telling me what I can and can't do. On the other hand, here was Vinnie Griso – this incredible man who was far beyond my even wildest dreams – telling me he had these Rules. And what's more, the Rules were there to protect me in case there was something I didn't want to do.

"Okay," I said finally. "Show me the Rules."

Chapter Five

I have to admit I'd never been in a situation like this before. Usually, when I meet a cute guy he might ask me out to a movie or maybe take me to the Olive Garden or something. Then maybe when he drives me home we might make out in his car for awhile or maybe I let him feel my boobs and then I go home and decide if I want to see him again or else he never calls and that's the end of it. That's usually the way it goes. Never, and I mean never, has a guy handed me a piece of paper – actually very old paper with fancy old-fashioned handwriting – with the Rules written out on them. But that's exactly what Vinnie Griso did.

Right there in his Secret Hideaway, he went over to this big old box that look like a pirate's treasure chest and unlocked it with what looked like a solid gold key. Then he pulls out this yellowed piece of parchment or whatever that has this whole bunch of Rules listed on it. He hands them to me and I started getting dizzy just looking at all those Rules. Even if I wanted to, how the hell was I going to remember all this shit? But then I looked over at Vinnie and he looked back at me like I was the most gorgeous woman on the face of the Earth and he wanted me more than anybody else in the world, so I decided I would at least read his damn Rules. Here they are:

Vinnie Griso's Extra Special Secret Rules

Rule Number One:
Vinnie is the "top." You are the "bottom" Don't ask any questions or else you might get hurt. Actually, you're going to get hurt whether you ask questions or not, so don't ask any questions.

Rule Number Two
You better do what Vinnie tells you to do or you're gonna really get hurt. And I mean it.

Rule Number Three
You're going to be asked to do some pretty weird sexual shit. It is vital that you enjoy it – or else. If you don't enjoy it, you better pretend to enjoy it. Plus you gotta be pretty good at pretending, because I can tell if you are faking it.

Rule Number Four
You better look fucking great at all times. That means put on makeup, eye shadow, mascara, shave your legs, tease your hair and do all the rest of that shit that broads do. I'll buy

you a lot of nice sexy and/or trashy clothes that you have to wear at all times, including at your niece's christening and whenever I take you to my friends' poker games.

Rule Number Five
Don't get fat! I don't give a shit how you do it, but if you get fat – and I mean gain one fucking ounce – I will beat the living crap out of you. (Note: This rule is an exception to the so-called "safe words" discussed later in these Rules)

Rule Number Six
No fooling around with other guys. And I mean it! If I catch you so much as talking to another guy, I will beat the living crap out of you. (See Rule Number Five. This Rule is also an exception to so-called "safe words")

Rule Number Seven
"Fooling around" in Rule Number Six includes kissing, fucking, hand jobs, blow jobs, 69, anal sex, oral sex, and any other kind of fucking sex at all, plus holding hands, talking to another guy or even friggin' looking at another guy. Got it?

Rule Number Eight
Failure to comply with any of the above Rules will result in punishment. We're talking some very heavy shit. Don't even ask.

As I read through Vinnie's Rules, I started to have some doubts about this whole relationship. I mean, on the one hand, most of his Rules seemed pretty reasonable. Okay, maybe I don't have a lot of experience with men, but it seemed like Vinnie's Rules were the same rules that most guys have for their girlfriends. And the good thing was that everything was spelled out right there in black and white from the beginning so there wouldn't be any confusion or anything.

On the other hand, having a bunch of Rules wasn't the most romantic deal in the world. Sure, I've read about those "pre-nup" agreements that the movie stars have and I heard this guy once on Oprah talk about how every woman ought to have a signed agreement with a guy before she makes a commitment. Maybe I'm old-fashioned, but I don't believe everything has to be spelled out in advance. That takes a lot of the mystery and excitement out of it.

I have to say that Vinnie was actually showing me a lot of respect by laying out his Rules in advance. How many women can say their boyfriends are so upfront and honest? Most guys will be all nice and take you to dinner at the Olive Garden and buy you flowers, but once they get you in the sack or move in with you, then they start cheating on you or criticizing you or beating the crap out of you. At least Vinnie is being honest up front about the whole thing.

Okay, so call me a hopeless romantic, but I'm not

sure I'm down with the whole Rules deal. Where are the flowers and the candy and the poetry? A girl has to have a little romance in her life, and just laying out a bunch of Rules in advance kind of spoils it. Plus, I can see from Vinnie's Rules that he's a sweet, honest guy and is respectful and ready to make a commitment, but does he really love me? Sure, he's jealous of other guys and wants me to look great, but does he really truly love me in his heart of hearts?

"You know how I said I would never force you to do anything you didn't want to do?" said Vinnie, breaking into my inner thoughts.

"Yes."

"Well, I wanted you to know that I meant it when I said that. I have what I call my 'hard limits.' Do you want to see them?"

"Sure," I answered. I'm glad he didn't ask me right away what I thought about the Rules, because I was confused, as you can probably tell.

So Vinnie handed me his "hard limits," all nicely written out on another piece of parchment paper. I gulped and started reading.

Vinnie Griso's Hard Limits

Hard Limit Number One
There are no hard limits. Hah-hah. Just kidding.

Hard Limit Number Two
I will not personally kill any member of your family unless they really piss me off.

Hard Limit Number Three
I will not intentionally damage any of your internal or external organs, but if I do accidentally, I am truly sorry and will pay full medical expenses up to a limit of $399, provided that the medical procedures are conducted by a foreign-born doctor of my choosing.

Hard Limit Number Four
I will abide by the following safe words:

"Stop it Vinnie, you're killing me."
That means that you're bleeding but not seriously injured and that we should keep doing whatever we're doing because it really turns you on.

"I mean it Vinnie, I'm calling the cops"
That means you should go slower with whatever you're doing because it really turns me on and I want it to last for like four hours.

"Vinnie, I feel like someone stuck an axe handle up my butt."
That means someone stuck an axe handle up your

butt and you better fucking enjoy it.

Silence.

If you don't say anything, I assume you are either really turned on or in a coma or something, in which case what's the point of "safe words?"

Boy, that's a lot there for a girl to consider. I was certainly going to have to think over this whole relationship with Vinnie. His "hard limits" seemed fair, but I wondered if there was any room at all for negotiation. So I gathered up my courage and asked him.

"So, Vinnie...?"

"Yes, Annabelle?"

"Is there any room for negotiation here?"

"By who?"

"By me."

"What did you have in mind?"

I had to think fast. I didn't really know where to begin. I'd never had to negotiate for anything like this before. I mean, maybe I bargained with the guy when I bought my used Kia that was a piece of shit anyway and died after like six weeks, but this was different. Real different.

"Well...like $399 doesn't seem like a helluva lot for medical expenses."

"You know, Annabelle, you're right. I'll go for $499."

"Really?"

"Yep, no problem."

Boy, Vinnie really was reasonable. I might have thought he was trying to take advantage of me or something, but I could see he just wanted to make me happy.

"Cool. So I have to do everything you tell me to?"

"That's right."

"What if you tell me to go jump in a lake?"

"Then you go jump in a lake."

"Would you rescue me?"

"Sure. You think I want you to drown?"

That sounded reasonable. Not that he would ever tell me to go jump in a lake. But if he did, I would of course. And he promised he'd rescue me. So that didn't seem like a problem.

"Um....what if I need to go to the bathroom and you won't let me go to the bathroom?"

"Why would I do that?"

"I don't know. Just say you did."

"Well, let's see. If you need to go to the bathroom and I won't let you go to the bathroom..."

"Right. What happens then?"

"In that case, I guess you pee in your pants."

That seemed fair enough I guess. But I still had another question.

"What if I had to go number 2? What would happen then?"

I could see Vinnie wasn't quite sure about that. He

was giving it a lot of thought. Finally, he scratched his head.

"Tell you the truth, I'm not quite sure."

"Would you let me go number 2?"

"You know, I can't say exactly for certain right now. And don't hold me to this. But I believe I would let you go to the bathroom for number 2 ."

"Even if you had told me before not to go to the bathroom?"

"Yeah, probably so."

See, I knew he was a reasonable guy. I can understand why it would be okay for me to piss in my pants if he told me not to go to the bathroom. And I could go along with that. But number 2? That was a stretch. But he agreed with me. From his answer, I could see that we were thinking alike about his Rules. In fact, I realized that Vinnie and I had a lot in common. He probably had a rough childhood, being the son of the one and only Vincent Griso, Sr. of Vinnie's Auto Parts fame. He probably got pushed around a lot by his dad and was teased at school and bullied. No wonder he had a chip on his shoulder.

But I could see inside Vinnie's rough exterior. No matter how messed up and perverted he might seem on the outside, I could tell that inside he had a warm and generous and loving heart. At that moment, I realized that inside that big, buff, gorgeous hunk of a body was a little boy who was looking desperately for love. True, some women might find all the whips and chains and stuff to be a turnoff – not to mention his weird Rules – but I saw all that as a challenge. I was going to make Vinnie Griso fall in love with me even if it meant my body was going to be black and blue all over. I knew that my mission from that moment forward would be to love, honor and obey – especially to obey – Mr. Vincent Griso, Junior.

Chapter Six

Only five minutes later, we're in Vinnie's bedroom, going at it hot and heavy. We're ripping each others' clothes off – I'm down to my pink panties and thong and he's in his all-black Calvin Kleins. I am so turned on I can't stand it, and I can see that Vinnie is ready to burst. Still, even though we're in the heat of passion and there's nothing on my mind except consumating my incredibly passionate and romantic love for Vinnie Griso, there was still one thing bothering me.

"Vinnie, hold on..." I panted, pulling away from his embrace.

"What the fuck?" he said, gasping for breath.

"I need to talk to you a second."

"Why?"

"Remember how you said we need to be honest with each other?"

"Yeah. So?"

"So I've got something I have to tell you."

He sighed and groaned.

"What is it?"

I didn't know exactly how to tell him, so I just blurted it out.

"Well, I'm not really that experienced....sexually."

"What the fuck??!!" he cried, jumping back like he'd seen a ghost. "You aren't a virgin are you?"

"No, nothing like that. It's just that I haven't been with that many guys."

"Like how many?"

"I don't know, maybe ten or twelve." I was lying of course. It was more like five or six, and most of those had been hand jobs or blow jobs. But I wasn't about to admit that to Vinnie.

"You're fucking kidding me!!"

"I'm afraid not."

"This is fucking crazy!"

"I'm sorry. I don't know what to say."

"I mean, you're blowing my mind here. When you walked into my office you looked like a total slut."

"I know, I know," I said, lowering my head in shame.

"You looked like you'd been done by hundreds of guys every which way and sideways. And now you tell me this?!"

"I didn't want to mislead you."

With that, he fixed me with a hard stare with his clear, cold blue eyes.

"Well you did."

"I'm sorry, Vinnie."

"What am I supposed to do? I thought you were this total 'ho, and now you tell me you're practically a virgin."

"But I'm not..." I protested.

"Okay. We'll see about that. So you fucked a bunch of guys, right?"

"Yeah, of course."

"How many?"

"A lot. A whole lot. And hard."

"How hard did you fuck them?"

"Very hard."

"No hand jobs?"

"A couple maybe. But very hard hand jobs. Very hard."

"Blow jobs?"

"Yeah. But tough. Very mean. Biting and every-thing."

"Okay, okay. Doggy style?"

"Definitely. Definitely doggy."

"You liked it?

"Are you kidding? I fucking loved it."

He paused and gave me an intense stare.

"Were you ever on top?"

I had to think before I answered that one. I figured him being a "top" and everything, Vinnie would get pissed off if I told him I liked it on top. Plus I couldn't remember if I'd ever actually been on top. Honestly, all of that stuff was a bit of blur, considering I was mostly drunk or stoned or extremely tired whenever I had sex.

"Oh, no. No way. I hate it on top."

"You sure?"

"Oh, yeah. Yuck! Fey! Gross! I'm definitely a 'bottom' kind of a girl."

"Really?" he said. I could tell he was intrigued. "How about anal sex?"

Okay, here we go. This was the rough part. I knew I had to lie about this

one. The closest I ever got to anal sex was when Freddy Gonzalez tried to stick his finger in my butt and I told him to shove it up his own ass. Except maybe for the time when I was playing doctor with my cousin Eileen and we stuck pencils up each others' tushes.

"Anal sex?"

"Yeah. Anal sex," said Vinnie, starting to pant again.

"Oh, definitely. All the time. Nothing but anal, anal, anal."

"Really?"

"Yeah, yeah. My butt is sore all the time. I'm always soaking it in the bathtub and my mom is yelling in 'What are you doing in there' and I tell her 'I'm soaking my sore butt.'"

Whenever I lie I start chewing the inside of my cheek. You'd think after all the lies I tell I'd stop doing it, but I just can't help it. So I start chewing on my cheek and

Vinnie looks at me.

"Don't do that," he says.

"What?"

"That," he says, pointing at my cheek. I can see that he is starting to get really turned on.

"Why not?" I say, kind of batting my eyelashes. "Is it turning you on?"

"Totally!" he says, and pushes me down on his bed. Apparently he believed me about all the guys I fucked doggy style and had anal sex with, or else he was so turned on he didn't care. Because in a flash, he was on top of me, running his hands through my hair and kissing my neck.

I don't think I ever had any guy kiss my neck like that before. He wasn't biting it or even sucking it, just kind of caressing it like it was the most erotic part of my body. And right then it was. I was moaning as he barely touched my neck with his lips and his tongue, then moving up to my earlobe, which he nudged softly with his nose and then took ever so softly between his lips and sucked.

OMG. This was going to be good! Vinnie was already totally different from any guy that I had been with. He was slow and soft and gentle as he kissed my neck and then went back to kissing my lips. It was like he was getting ready to enjoy every inch of me, like I was this incredible feast for his eyes and his lips. Slowly he unfastened my bra, rolling me to the side as my breasts sort of spilled out. Then he stopped and just stared at my boobs. I looked up at him, alarmed.

"Is something wrong?"

"You are just so beautiful," he said breathlessly.

OhmyGod I don't think anybody ever said that to me – at least not in the way Vinnie did at that moment. I was almost dizzy with excitement. Seeing him staring at my breasts with such lust and passion in his eyes made me so turned on that I wanted him right now. But he was going to take his sweet time, I could tell.

He took his hand and softly cupped one of my breasts. Feeling the warmth of his hand on my breast sent shivers of excitement all over my body. I couldn't help it – my eyes closed and I let out a soft moan. When I opened my eyes again, Vinnie was smiling. He lowered his head toward my breast and slowly licked around the nipple. It was like a jolt of electricity shot through my whole body. I had never felt anything like that before, and he had only just begun.

He was toying with my nipple now – licking, sucking, biting until I could barely stand it anymore. I held his head in my hands, running my fingers through his beautiful mane of black hair, and pressed him tighter to my breasts. It was like I was on a roller coaster ride, going up and up, then plummeting down as he caressed my breasts.

Slowly, he worked his way down from my breasts to my stomach, lightly flicking his tongue all around the skin, which felt like it was alive with all these crazy sensations.

He kissed my belly button and then blew lightly on it. It was almost like a gentle tickle that turned into this fabulous sensation of passion and lust. His tongue traced a line lower down, across my stomach, my hips and my thighs. I was desperate to take off my panties, and tried to pull them off but he stopped me.

"Wait," he whispered.

"But...?" I was so friggin' turned on I couldn't wait one more second.

"Wait..." he said again.

So I lay back and tried to hold myself back from grabbing his head and pushing it between my thighs.

Very slowly, he took my thong between his teeth and pulled it down, across my hips and down to my knees. Okay, I've seen stuff like that in the movies, but until a guy does this, you cannot believe how sexy it is. It's like this sensation of a male animal slowly making love to a female animal, using everything in his power, including his teeth. After he had slowly pulled my thong off, he rested his head between my thighs and stopped. He could sense that he was staring at my pussy, which made me feel a little uncomfortable, but it also got me even wetter.

"Your pussy is amazing," he murmured.

I never really thought that my pussy was amazing. I mean I'd checked it out in the mirror and everything and I guess it looked okay. I never thought about it much until right then. Amazing? Vinnie Griso thinks my pussy is amazing? I could feel like an electric shock go from my pussy right to my brain and then back again about a million times. I am so hot for this guy I can't even think.

"I want you...now." I moaned.

"What do you want?" he asked with a smile.

"I want you to fuck me...now!"

"Oh, no. Not yet."

I felt like screaming FUCK ME! But I was also enjoying having him in between my thighs, staring adoringly at my pussy. Then he moved his lips closer, running them along the inside of my thighs and brushing his soft hair against the outside of my pussy. Jesus...

He stopped for a moment, and then, very slowly, he ran the tip of his tongue up the length of my pussy lips. I groaned with pleasure. Then he did it again, gently and deliberately. My pussy was throbbing and gushing with excitement, but he was taking his time, torturing me with his tongue, licking me up and down the length of my pussy, inside and out, up and down, teasing my clit, and sending out jolts of pleasure through my whole body until I couldn't stand it anymore.

"Oh, please..." I pleaded. I knew I was ready to come at any moment, and I wanted him inside of me.

Vinnie pulled his mouth away from my pussy and looked up at me with a very happy grin on his face. Then he stood up slowly next to the bed and gazed down at me, still writhing with pleasure. I couldn't take my eyes off his body.

His broad, strong shoulders, his well-muscled stomach and thighs. And there, still hidden inside his Calvin Klein -- a captivating bulge. Just looking at it made me even more aroused.

I couldn't stop myself from reaching out and caressing the outside of his briefs. I could even feel his penis throbbing through the soft material. I slowly pulled down his Calvins until it popped out in all its glory. And it was glorious – large, throbbing and eager. I ran my finger up its length and felt it pulsating, then I gently ran my tongue up and down as Vinnie began to moan.

It made me feel powerful, even as I wanted to surrender myself completely to Vinnie – to have him bury this beautiful cock inside me and touch me in all the places I was aching to be touched. As I wrapped my lips around the head of his cock, he gave a little gasp, then pushed me a little further down. I could taste the saltiness at the tip of his cock and smell the all the sexiness of his body. My pussy was pounding with excitement as I took more of his cock into my mouth.

After a moment, he pulled my head away and pushed me forcefully back onto the bed. As he looked down at me, I felt his animal passion and wanted only to be part of him – to have him deep inside me. He took his cock and teased it along the lips of my pussy, rubbing it gently against my clit until I was ready to scream.

"Please, please..." I begged.

Slowly he pushed the head of his penis a little way inside me as waves of pleasure started to crash over me. He pulled it out, then in again, each time sending more and more shocks through my body. I was swooning as he pushed harder and harder, with a rhythm that felt like jolts of ecstasy with each thrust. I felt myself melting into the joy of his body, gripping his cock as it grew even harder, pounding into me with a passionate urgency.

Orgasm.

"Oh, God..." I groaned as my pussy began to pulsate as my whole body buckled and grasped him into him.

"OH...GOD!!" I cried out, gripping his cock with my pussy as he plunged again and again, finally releasing himself in a huge flood of pleasure as we melted together.

Orgasm.

It was like I had died and gone to heaven. I rested for a moment, quietly in his arms. I felt this amazing peace come over me. I had given myself to Vinnie Griso completely and totally, like I never had before. I wanted to stay this way in his arms forever. But suddenly my bliss was interrupted by a voice from outside the bedroom.

"Vincent??"

Vinnie looked over at me with panic in his eyes.

"OhmyGod" he cried, jumping out of bed.

"Who is it?" I said, wondering who would have the balls to interrupt us at a time like this.

He looked at me with a pained expression on his

face.

"My mother," he said glumly.

Chapter Seven

I don't think I've ever gotten dressed so fast in my whole life. Vinnie and I were throwing our clothes on as fast as we could. I probably looked like a total wreck after the last hour of blissful passion in the sack with Vinnie, but I tried to at least straighten out my hair and make sure my blouse wasn't on backward. Vinnie looked almost as panicked as I did. He was pulling on his pants as fast as he could and quickly buttoning his shirt.

"Vinnie?" came his mother's shrill voice from outside the bedroom. "Are you decent?"

I looked over at him.

"Do you want me to hide?" I asked.

He thought for a minute and shook his head.

"No, it's okay."

"Do I look alright?"

He gave me quick kiss.

"You look gorgeous."

Even though his mother was right outside the door, I felt like fucking him all over again right there.

"Vinnie! I'm coming in!"

If that voice didn't break the spell, I don't know what would. Next thing I know Vinnie opens the door and in comes his mother, all five foot three, two hundred pounds of her. She's wearing a tight, low-cut cocktail black dress – I guess the whole family has a thing for black – and she's kind of swerving like she's been drinking. Plus she's carrying something in a big shopping bag.

At first, she doesn't see me, and goes right over to Vinnie and lays a big, fat slobbery kiss on his lips. I have this sudden fear that she's going to smell my pussy on him but the whole thought of that grosses me out and so I put it right out of my mind. Then she gives him a big hug and hands him the shopping bag.

"I brought you chicken wings. I know they're your favorite."

"Thanks, Ma. But you didn't have to," he says sheepishly.

"Come on. What are mothers for?" she says, and gives him a slap on the butt. Just then, she turns around and sees me. I'm kind of cowering off to the side hoping to disappear. She stares at me for a moment, then turns to Vinnie.

"I didn't know you had company."

"Ma, this is Annabelle Stilletto."

She eyes me up and down, then puts out her hand.

"Nice to meet you, Annabelle."

"My pleasure, Mrs. Griso."

She gives me a fake smile and turns to Vinnie.

"Is this your new 'bottom?'"

Vinnie turns red and I feel all the blood draining out of my brain.

"Ma!"

"I'm sorry. I'm just asking."

"It's none of your business."

"Okay, okay. But, you know, mothers can tell what's going on. They have this sixth sense. Right, Annabelle?"

I didn't know what to say. I just stared at the floor.

"Listen," she said, giving me a pat on the back, "you don't have nothing to be ashamed of. As long as you make my Vinnie happy, that's all I care. You're both grown up. Consenting adults. How old are you, dear?"

"Twenty-four," I say, not looking up.

"See, you're old enough to decide for yourself. If you and Vinnie want to play 'Master and Slave,' it's totally up to you."

"Ma!!"

"Sorry. Excuse me for living. I'll change the subject." She turns back to me. "You like chicken wings?"

I glance over at Vinnie.

"Sure, I guess."

"Okay, dig in. Let's have a party."

Vinnie looks over at me.

"Ma, we're kind of busy right now."

"What? You playing with your whips and chains?"

"Okay, Ma. That's enough."

"I'm just kidding. You can't take a joke?" She gives me a nudge. "He was always real sensitive. His father used to call him a 'Momma's boy.' Are you a 'Momma's boy,' Vinnie?"

She gives him a pinch on the cheek. He rolls his eyes.

"No, Ma."

"Okay, maybe just a little bit," she says with a smile. "Anyways," she continues, digging into the chicken wings, "his father was a real sonofabitch. Used to beat the shit out of him for crying. One time this bully beat Vinnie up at school so his Dad made him get boxing gloves so he could teach him how to box. I think it was just an excuse for his Dad to beat the crap out of him. What a sonofabitch."

"Okay, Ma. That's enough."

"Oh, yeah. I forgot. You've got to work with the bastard. Mr. Vincent Griso of the famous Vinnie's Auto Parts. He should go fuck himself. Lousy bastard. Ran off with his secretary right under my nose. But you know what? I'm happier. Much happier. I got a coupla million bucks out of the sonofabitch. It wasn't easy, but I sued his ass. Now I got a boyfriend only a coupla years older than Vinnie here. Bobby Mendoza. The guy is built like a brick shit house and hung like a horse, if you know what I saying."

"Ma...."

"Uh-oh. I'm offending Vinnie here. Like I said he's

sensitive. You want some more chicken wings?"

She holds out a couple of chicken wings dripping with barbecue sauce. I have to admit, after all the lovemaking with Vinnie, I was pretty hungry and the chicken wings looked damned good.

"Sure," I said, chomping down on a juicy chicken wing.

"The girl's got an appetite. That's a good sign, Vinnie. If you know what I mean."

She gives me a wink. I can't help giggling.

"Plus a sense of humor. Hey, Vinnie, she could be a keeper."

There was something about this lady I was starting to like. I mean, she was pretty crude and all that, but I could tell that she had a good heart. And it looked like she was a good mother, although I could tell that Vinnie was pissed off at her. I can understand, since nobody wants your mother barging in when you're right in the middle of hot sex, but you have to admit that bringing chicken wings right to his house was pretty sweet.

"So, Daisy Bell..."

"...It's Annabelle," I interrupted.

"Sorry, Annabelle. So how long have you known my son here?"

I thought for a moment.

"About ten hours."

"No kidding. He moves pretty fast, doesn't he?"

"Ma!"

"Sorry. Excuse me for living."

"I went for a job interview with him this morning, and one thing led to another."

"No shit. Has he showed you the Rules yet?"

"MA!!"

"Come on. What's the big deal? We're all adults here. Nobody cares what you do in the privacy of your own bedroom."

I hesitated, looking over to Vinnie. He just stared down at the floor. So I figured what the hell.

"Yeah," I said softly. "He showed them to me."

"So? What do you think?"

"I'm not sure."

"What? You don't think you can do what my son wants?"

"It's not that."

"What then? You don't want to make him happy?"

"Of course I do."

"So then what's the problem?"

"Well, I'm not sure I can obey all the Rules."

"Why not?"

"Because I'm not so good at obeying Rules."

"Hey, it's easy. Just do what Vinnie tells you and you'll be fine."

"What if I don't want to do what he tells me?"

Vinnie and his mother both fix me with cold stares.

Then she turns to Vinnie.

"I thought she was supposed to be a 'bottom.'"

"She is," said Vinnie.

"Then what's the deal. You're the top, she's the bottom. She does what you tell her."

"Hold on a sec..." I blurt out.

"Shut up and let Vinnie talk," she snaps.

"It's complicated, Ma."

"What is so complicated?"

"She doesn't have a lot of experience."

"So?"

He lowers his voice, hoping I won't hear.

"I have to train her."

"Train me!!??" I cry. "Is that what this is all about??"

"No," says Vinnie.

"All this time when we were making love just now you were training me? Is that what was going on?"

"Not exactly..."

"Then what exactly was going on?" I screamed, throwing down my chicken wing.

"I'm very attracted to you, Annabelle."

"And I'm attracted to you, Vinnie," I replied, my lip quivering. "But I'm not about to let some guy – no matter how attractive he is – train me to be his 'bottom!'"

"Why the hell not?" said his mother. "It doesn't sound so bad to me."

"But what about love?" I cried.

"What about it?" she replied.

"I thought he loved me."

"He probably does. Or he will. Don't worry about it for now. Just do what he tells you and everything will be alright."

"I don't think so," I said, my lip quivering as I was about to cry. "I think all of this was a really big mistake."

With that, I turned bright red with anger. I couldn't believe what was happening. Here I'd had the most incredible night of my life and Vinnie's mother was ruining everything. Plus, I can't believe he told her that he was "training" me. Didn't he have any respect for me at all?

"Annabelle," said Vinnie, reaching out to grab my arm.

"Don't touch me, okay?" I said, pulling my arm away. "I'm leaving. And I don't want to have anything to do with you – or your mother – again!"

With that, I stormed out the door. As I was leaving, I could hear Vinnie and his mother start to argue.

"Look what you did, Ma?"

"What? Did I say something wrong?"

"You scared her away."

"Aw, she was trash anyway."

So that's what they think of me? I'm some piece of trash he can pick up and throw away when he's done with me? Just because he's this rich, hot guy with a gorgeous body who wants to buy me anything I want. As I ran out of the house, tears began streaming down my cheeks.

Chapter Eight

I stumbled out of Vinnie's mansion and realized I was in the middle of fucking Alpine, New Jersey with no idea how I was going to get home. As I stood there weeping in the driveway of the mansion. Vinnie came running after me. I could tell he was really upset but there was no way I was going back in there.

"Annabelle, wait!"

I stopped and turned around to face him.

"Look, I'm really sorry," he said. "Ma says a lot of stupid things sometimes."

I didn't want to even talk to him, but I was so angry I had to say something.

"I can deal with your mother. It's what you said that pissed me off."

"I know, it was stupid."

"It was more than stupid, Vinnie. It was incredibly disrespectful."

"I know, I know. And I'm sorry. I didn't mean it."

"Yes, you did."

"Annabelle, I care for you. A lot. Don't you realize that?"

"If that's how you talk to people you care for, then you know what? Fuck you!"

With that, I turned and headed up the driveway.

"Wait! Where are you going?"

"Home!" I said angrily.

"How are you going to get there?"

Good question. I had no idea. But I certainly wasn't going to stay here.

"Let me at least have T-Bomb take you home."

"Thanks, but I can get there on my own."

"Don't be stupid, Annabelle, it's the middle of the night. You can't get a taxi to come all the way out here. Let T-Bomb drive you."

Of course, he was right. I was stranded. God knows how I was going to get back to Jersey City at this hour. I stopped. I had no choice.

"Okay, I accept the offer."

"Thank you."

"But let me tell you this, Vinnie Griso. I never want to see you or hear from you again. Is that clear?"

Vinnie paused for a moment, staring at me intently.

"We'll see about that."

"No, we won't. This is definitely goodbye."

With that, I strode over to his limo, which by now had pulled up beside us. T-Bomb was holding the door open and I got in without saying a word and then promptly burst into tears. I cried all the way home. Now and then, T-Bomb would try to make me feel better, but it didn't do any good. All I could think about was how wonderful the evening had been – a beautiful dinner in Vinnie's incredible mansion followed by the most spectacular lovemaking of my entire life. How could he say those things to me after what we had shared?

I was like a limp dishrag full of tears when T-Bomb let me out in front of my apartment building. I could hardly walk up the front stoop and get the key in the front door. By the time I made it inside the apartment, I collapsed on the couch and started bawling my eyes out. Naturally, I woke up Shelly who came out of her bedroom, half-asleep.

"What happened, Annabelle?"

I could hardly get the words out. I was stammering and stuttering and blubbering.

"He...I...it was...I'm so...humiliated...I can't believe..."

"What are you talking about?"

"Vinnie...He..."

"Okay, slow down. Start at the beginning."

I was trying to regain my composure, but at the same time I was crying and hyperventilating.

"I went..."

"You went to his house."

"Right."

"What was it like?"

"Fucking...humongous," I said in between sobs.

"That's cool."

"Yes....very cool," I said, sobbing even more.

"So you went to his humongous house."

"It was a mansion!" I wailed.

"Okay, it was a mansion. Then what?"

"We had....dinner."

"Alright. How was that?"

"It was....amazing."

"Sounds okay so far. What happened next?"

"He took me...into this like...secret room."

"Uh-oh. He didn't rape you, did he?"

"No!"

"Good. So what's in this secret room?"

"Oh, you know, a lot of stuff. Whips. Chains. Stuff like that."

"Holy shit, Annabelle. Is this guy some kind of sadist?"

"Not exactly. Well, sort of."

"What do you mean 'sort of'?"

"He has these Rules."

"What kind of Rules?"

"Rules that I am supposed to obey."

"This doesn't sound good."

"It's not that bad really. He just wants to take care of me."

"And boss you around."

"Yeah."

"Because he gets off on that."

"It gives him pleasure."

"Fuck that. I'll give him some fucking pleasure!"

"It's not what you think, Shel."

"Oh, no? He's got you in his secret room with a bunch of crazy Rules. What am I supposed to think?"

"I think he really cares about me."

"Annabelle, you've known the guy one day."

"I know. But we have this connection."

"I've heard that shit before."

"Not from me."

She shook her head in disbelief. I could tell she was judging me. But I needed for her to understand everything I was feeling.

"Okay, so tell me what happened next."

"We made love."

"With whips and chains?"

"No. It was normal."

"Normal?"

"Actually, it was incredible. Shel, I have never felt anything like that with a guy. I can hardly describe it. It was like something out of the movies – even better. I was so turned on and we were so connected and I have never felt anything like that before."

"He has a nice body?"

"Gorgeous."

"Big dick?"

"More than big."

"So he's good in bed?"

"Amazing."

I could see Shelly was getting a little more curious about Vinnie. I wondered if might be jealous that I had met this gorgeous, rich guy who was great in bed and was sending me into ecstasy while she was at home with her doofus boyfriend watching pornos on the couch.

"Okay. So what is the problem? Is it the whips and chains?"

"Yeah, partly."

"I should say so."

"But it gets worse."

"Worse than whips and chains?"

"Uh-huh."

"Do tell."

"So after we finish making love, we're lying there in his bedroom. And I'm feeling incredibly close to him and connected and all warm and fuzzy..."

"Okay, I get it, I get it," said Shelly. I could tell she was getting annoyed with all the stuff about what a great lover Vinnie was.

"Then, all of sudden, his mother shows up."

"His mother?"

"Yep. She brought chicken wings."

"Chicken wings?"

"Uh-huh. They were actually pretty good."

"Hold it. You were in bed with her son and she shows up with chicken wings?"

"Yep. Kinda sweet, don't you think?"

"No," snapped Shelly. "It's fucking crazy. What did you do?"

"I ate a couple of chicken wings and we all talked."

"About what?"

"Well, that's the bad part. She asked Vinnie if I was his new 'bottom.'"

"What's a 'bottom'?"

"You know, how in a relationship there's a 'top' and a 'bottom.'"

"In a fucked-up relationship you mean."

"I guess."

"So you're the 'bottom'?"

"No! His mother thought I was the 'bottom.'"

"Vinnie's new 'bottom'?"

"Uh-huh."

"Annabelle, this is very fucked up. First of all, do you really want to be some guy's 'bottom'? I don't care how rich or gorgeous he might be, is that really what you want? Plus, his mother is asking you if you're the new 'bottom.' How fucked up is that?"

"It did seem kinda strange."

"Strange? It's sick."

"I guess. But she said we're consenting adults and we should be able to do what we want."

"It's his mother, Annabelle! Think about that for a second."

"Okay, okay. I get your point. Still, I wasn't that upset. I figured she was his mother and only wanted him to be happy."

"I'll bet she did."

"What really got me pissed was what Vinnie said."

"What did he say?"

"He said he was 'training' me."

"Vinnie said that?"

"Yep."

"Annabelle, you gotta dump this guy. Right now. That is fucking crazy."

"I know, I know. So I left right away but I didn't have any way to get home so his limo driver gave me a ride. Still, I can't help thinking about him. It's like we have something really special."

"Yeah, 'special.' The guy wants to beat the shit out of you."

"At least he's honest about it. Most guys treat you real nice until you go to bed with them or move in or something and then they beat the shit out of you."

"That's not true, Annabelle."

"Okay, maybe not. Maybe your boyfriend doesn't beat you up. He just sits around and watches pornos on the couch."

"He's looking for work!"

"Oh yeah, right."

"This is bullshit, Annabelle."

"Okay, Shel. I'm sorry. It's just that Vinnie is so sweet and I know he's looking for someone special to love."

"A special 'bottom' you mean."

"It's not like he's looking to beat the crap out of me. His Rules are very clear about that."

"Oh yeah? Like how?"

"It's all about pleasure."

"His pleasure."

"Okay, but what's wrong with making him happy?"

"I can't believe you're saying this."

"Look, I'm not going to see him anymore. Okay?"

"Promise?"

"Promise. All I'm saying is that he's not that bad a guy."

"He's a creep, Annabelle. Face it. A rich and gorgeous creep, maybe. But still a creep."

"I don't want to argue with you anymore."

Shelly looked at me sadly and stroked my hair.

"You better get some sleep, okay?"

"Okay."

I have to admit I was pretty tired. After the all the emotions of the day, I was ready to collapse. So I changed into my nightgown and lay down in the darkness of my bedroom. As tired as I was, I still couldn't fall asleep right away. I keep thinking about Vinnie Griso and his clear blue eyes and his gorgeous black hair.

Chapter Nine

The next morning I'm having this beautiful dream about me and Vinnie. We're in his bedroom making love and I'm getting incredibly hot and he's telling me how beautiful and gorgeous I am and I'm looking deep into his clear blue eyes and he's telling me how much he loves me and suddenly J-Lo is singing...

Let your rhythm change the world on the floor

I'm still dreaming but this time it's his mother and she's ringing the doorbell and she's got this whole shopping cart full of chicken wings.

Let your rhythm change the world on the floor

Now I'm hearing her voice and she's yelling, "Vinnie! VINNIE!!"

Let your rhythm change the world on the floor

I wake up with a jolt and I'm in a cold sweat. My head is throbbing and my pussy is sore from the night before. And still I'm hearing this noise from next to my bed.

Let your rhythm change the world on the floor

Shit, it's my cell phone alert tone of J-Lo and Pitbull

singing On the Floor – my latest fav tune. There's a whole bunch of text messages and voice mails all backed up. And every one of them is from Vinnie. Here are just a few:

"r u ok?"
"miss u!!"
"SOOOORRRRYYY!!!"
"we have to talk!"
"call me!!!!!!"

I clicked over to my voice mail. Same thing. Dozens of messages:

"Hi Annabelle. It's Vinnie. I'm really sorry about last night. I can't believe I was so stupid and hurt you like that. I really need to talk to you. Call me back."

"It's Vinnie. I really miss you and I'm so sorry. Let me make it up to you. Call me."

"It's me. I know you're ignoring my calls, but I have to talk to you. Call me."

"Hey. Just give me another chance, okay? I want to make it up to you. Big time."

"Annabelle. Call me. I mean it. I gotta talk to you!"

I got up, still groggy, and went into the bathroom and plopped down on the toilet. What was I going to do? Vinnie had really treated me bad, but I knew deep down that we had this strong connection. Of course, his whole Rules thing was weird, but everybody's got issues, right? Still, I promised Shelly I wouldn't talk to him or see him again, so I didn't know what to do. I felt badly because I knew he really missed me and was sorry and everything. He probably just wanted a chance to explain and make it up to me.

Okay, so I promised Shelly I wouldn't see him or talk to him, but what harm could it do to text him? I knew he felt bad and I should at least give him a chance to apologize. That way we could end in on a better note, and we could both get on with our lives. I wouldn't have to see him or anything, he could just send me an email or maybe we could talk for a little while on the phone. It didn't seem like there would be anything wrong with that, right?

So I texted him while I was sitting there on the toilet:

"I dont want to talk to u."

I hit send and started to cry. How come everything had to be so complicated? Here was this really cute guy that I was very attracted to. He was rich and we had great sex. How come I was so worried about the whole Rules thing? What difference should that make if he really cares about me? And what is so wrong with giving some pleasure to another person, even if it does seem a little weird?

Let your rhythm change the world on the floor

It was Vinnie. He answered right away. I didn't know whether to be pissed or happy. I glanced at the text.

"but I really want to talk to u."

Shit! I could tell he was really hurting, but I didn't know what to do. Should I text him back or call him or what? I thought about asking Shelly, but I knew exactly what she'd say, so I texted him back.

"I cant talk to u."

Two seconds later...

"why not?"
"because Im busy"

I waited another two seconds. My phone rang. It's gotta be Vinnie. So what am I supposed to do? Just ignore it? He'll just call again. And again.

"Hello"
"It's me."
"Yeah. What?"

"Listen, I'm really sorry about last night."

"Me, too."

"No, really. I know what I said was horrible. You didn't deserve it."

"No shit."

"It's my mother. She makes me crazy."

"So you're blaming your mother?"

"No, no. It's completely my fault. I was a jerk. Just believe me that I didn't want to hurt you."

"Not until you train me first, right?"

"Annabelle..."

I started to cry.

"How could you treat me that way? I thought we had this special connection."

"We do."

"Are you just saying that?"

"Of course not."

"Really?"

"Really."

I was still sniffling but didn't want to hang up. Despite everything, I wanted to hear Vinnie's voice.

"Can I see you?" he asked.

"I don't know..."

"But why not?"

"It doesn't seem like a good idea."

"It does to me."

Vinnie was being very persuasive, and just hearing

his voice made me soften. I knew he cared about me, and maybe I was willing to at least meet with him and clear the air. Otherwise, I might spend the rest of my life wondering what might have been.

"Where would we meet?"

"Anywhere you like."

I thought about it. I definitely didn't want to go back to his house. And meeting at some bar or restaurant could be weird, especially if we wanted to talk about what had happened between us.

"How about your office?"

"Fine."

I figured that would be safe. There were plenty of people around, but we could still shut the door and talk. What could possibly go wrong?

"When should we meet?"

"How about this afternoon?"

I was seized with this fear in my stomach. This afternoon? I wasn't sure I was ready for this. After all, I promised Shelly I wasn't going to see him again.

"I don't know…"

"It'll be okay."

"You sure?"

"Absolutely. I promise. How about five o'clock?"

"Okay."

"I'll have T-Bomb pick you up."

"No, that's okay. I'll take the bus."

"Are you sure?"

"Yeah."

I know it would have been a lot easier to go in his limo, but after last night, I wanted to feel like I could get there on my own.

"Okay. I'll see you here at five."

"Okay."

"Promise?"

"I promise."

"I can't wait to see you. You don't know how much I've missed you."

"Really?"

"Really."

I was melting. I could feel it. I was dissolving right into the bathroom floor like the Wicked Witch of the West. I was nothing but a puddle of tears right there next to the bathtub.

"Goodbye, " he said softly.

"'Bye," I said, but I was already in another world. All I could think about was those clear blue eyes gazing down at my naked body with lust and adoration. I knew I was in big trouble when Shelly knocked on the bathroom door.

"What are you doing in there?"

"Nothing."

"Were you talking to somebody on the phone?"

I paused.

"...No"

With that, Shelly barged in the door.

"Were you talking to him?"

"No, of course not."

"You're lying."

"Okay, I was talking to him."

"Why? You promised you wouldn't"

"I know, but he was so sad and upset."

"Upset my ass. The guy's a creep and he treated you bad."

"I know. But I didn't want to end it like that."

"Just as long as you end it."

"I will."

"What do you mean 'I will?' Didn't you end it already?"

"Not exactly."

"Shit, Annabelle."

"He wants to see me."

"Of course he wants to see you. He wants to beat the crap out of you."

"Will you stop saying that?"

"Did you agree to see him? Don't tell me you're going to see him?"

I nodded.

"You're hopeless."

"I know, I know. But I wanted to give him one more chance."

"How about giving yourself a chance?"

"Shel, he's not that bad."

"Oh no?"

"You don't know him. Besides, he could be the one."

"Oh yeah? How do you know?"

"Because there's something special about him?"

"Right. Specially weird."

"I don't want to argue about this, okay?'

"It's your life. But I'm your friend, Annabelle. I don't want you to get hurt."

"Thanks, Shel. But I'm okay."

"I hope so."

With that, Shelly gave me a hug. I told her I was okay, but I wasn't totally sure. I knew that Vinnie and I had this special chemistry, and I'd never felt that way about anybody else. But I also wasn't sure I could handle him – especially his Rules.

I took a shower and got dressed, changing my outfits three or four times in the process. I wanted to look attractive – and yes, sexy – but not trashy. I was still stinging from his mom's comment that I was "trash." Of course, I didn't want to look like some "plain Jane" – that's just not me. So I layered on the lipstick and mascara and teased my hair up a ways. If it was going to be over, I wanted Vinnie to get a good look at what he was going to be missing.

I got out of the apartment by about 4:15. It would take an hour on the bus but I wanted to make Vinnie wait for awhile. I made it past the dumb punks on the corner who were whistling at me and making gross comments. Even though I hated those punks, they were kind of like a test of how I was looking. If they didn't whistle and shout at me, maybe I needed to ramp up my act a little, if you know what I mean. But today, they whistled like always. I think it was the short, tight skirt – one of my favorites – that did the trick.

The Number 5 bus was late as usual but that gave me time to have a cigarette. I had given up smoking a couple of weeks earlier, but this whole Vinnie thing got me right back puffing away. I have to admit, I missed it. Something about sucking on a Virginia Slim made me feel real sexy, which I needed right now. When the bus finally arrived, it was full of a bunch of gross people – disgusting fat old ladies, homeless guys and street punks. I couldn't find a seat, of course, so I had to stand there while some creep stared at my butt. He looked like he was going to cop a quick feel, so I was ready to bash him hard across the jaw. About halfway there, I finally got a seat and was able to relax a little bit and think about what I was going to say to Vinnie.

The last couple of days had been such a whirlwind, I didn't know what to think. Only a little while ago, I was broke, with no job and nothing but a degree from Beauty School and an advanced certificate in Hair Styling. I'd had a couple of lame boyfriends who were jerks and no great boyfriend prospects. Then I met Vinnie, and suddenly my world opened up. A fantastic job, a new wardrobe, a furnished condo and a brand new car. What was I complaining about?

Okay, so Vinnie had some sexual weirdness going on. I know that's a little strange. But, after all, he was being honest with me. His Rules were a kind of harsh maybe, but maybe I could use some discipline in my life. Still, his mother was a major bitch and he was disrespecting me. How come he didn't tell his mother to fuck off? And what's the deal about "training" me. I don't need a guy running my life or turning me into some kind of sexual slave? All this was running through my brain as I sat on the bus with the fat ladies and the punks and the homeless guys. By the time I got off the bus in front of the world headquarters of Vinnie's Auto Parts, I still hadn't decided what I was going to do.

Chapter Ten

The security guard at the reception desk recognized me when I walked in. I guess he remembered me from the last time I was there, since he had definitely checked me out pretty good. Or else Vinnie's secretary had told him to expect me. Anyways, when I came up to the desk he greeted me with a big smile.

"Good afternoon, Miss Stilletto."

I was surprised that he remembered my name. Actually, I was kind of flattered. Like I was getting special VIP attention.

"Good afternoon."

"Mr. Griso, Junior is expecting you. You can go right up."

"Thanks," I said and gave him a smile. I was starting to feel better already.

The guard actually escorted me over to the elevator and made sure I got in okay. I could get used to this kind of treatment. When I got off the elevator on the third floor, Vinnie's secretary was waiting for me.

"Hello, Miss Stilletto. So nice to see you again."
This girl was practically kissing my feet.

"Nice to see you, too." Obviously, Vinnie had told them to be real good to me.

"Come with me. Mr. Griso is waiting for you."

With that, I could feel my heart start to race. I was excited to see Vinnie, but I didn't want to seem too eager. After all, he had treated me real bad, and I wasn't sure I could ever forgive him. This could be the last time I ever saw him, and I didn't want to act stupid or cry or anything. When we got to his office, I could feel my knees shaking. It seemed like such a long time ago that we were making love and he was turning my world upside down. I didn't know what was going to happen when I saw him, or even how I would feel.

But the minute I opened the door to his office and saw him standing there in his tight black pants with his black shirt unbuttoned and his jet black hair and his clear blue eyes, I started to melt. And then I looked around the office and saw that it was filled with beautiful flowers -- dozens and dozens of roses that I knew were meant especially for me. As our eyes met, I felt like rushing into his arms, but I stopped myself.

"Hello," I said quietly.

"Hello," he said. "I'm so glad you came."

I didn't say anything right away, but still managed to tear my eyes away from him.

"Pretty flowers," I said softly.

"They're all for you."

I smiled at him.

"They're beautiful."

"Annabelle..."

"Yes?"

"I am so sorry. I didn't mean to hurt you. It was stupid."

All I could do was nod as my eyes filled with tears.

"You know I respect you," he continued. "And would never hurt you."

"But what about your Rules?"

"I only want them if you want them."

"What does that mean?"

"You don't have to agree to anything you don't want to do."

"Really?"

"Absolutely. All I want is to give you pleasure and happiness."

Suddenly, it was as if all my anger and hurt melted away in a flash. My eyes welled up with tears and I rushed over to him. He took me in his arms and held me very tight.

"Annabelle," he whispered. "I'm so glad you came back."

"Me, too," I said, laughing through my tears.

I had always heard that so-called "make-up sex" was really fantastic, but I never believed it until a few minutes later when Vinnie and I were ripping each others' clothes off. I guess there is something about having a fight and then being mad at somebody and then making up that creates this incredible sexual energy. Boy, I could feel it!

Anyways, Vinnie had this room next to his office that you could only get to through a secret entrance in his private bathroom. It was like the Secret Room in his mansion, only smaller. But it still had all the stuff like whips and chains and handcuffs – which I was actually starting to get used to seeing. Also, it was soundproof so I didn't have to worry about making a lot of noise when we had sex. And I was definitely going to be making a lot of noise!

I was so turned on I couldn't wait. Vinnie was kissing every inch of my body, running his tongue up and down my neck and my breasts and my tummy until I was ready to scream. I couldn't get enough of him as he grabbed my ass and almost frantically pulled me toward him. His strong hands on my butt drove me wild and when he went down on his knees and buried his face in my pussy, all I could think about was having him inside me.

But he wasn't ready to give me that immediate satisfaction. He licked at my pussy, teasing my clit with his tongue until I was practically exploding. Then he stood up, grabbed both my arms, spun me around and pushed me against the wall. I was kind of scared about what he might do, but I was so turned on that all I could do was plead with him to fuck me.

Still, he kept teasing me, playing with my pussy and my nipples even as he pressed me even harder against the wall. I could feel his cock against me, throbbing and pulsating, and I just wanted him inside me – now! I reached over to grab his cock, but he pulled my hand away and murmured "Not yet."

"Oh, please..." I moaned.

"Not yet," he said, even more firmly.

Then he pulled both my hands behind my back and held them tightly. He spread my legs apart and slowly ran the tip of his cock between my legs, brushing against the lips of my pussy and then resting for a moment against my clit. His cock felt huge and hot against me and I tried to push against him to force his cock inside me. But he kept on teasing me, putting the very tip of his cock a little bit inside, and then pulling it out. Again and again, he teased me like that, until finally he thrust inside me so deep that I let a loud shriek and pushed against him as hard as I could.

Orgasm.

Waves and waves of pleasure swept over me, like nothing I had ever felt before. That got Vinnie even more excited and hard, and I was already way over the top. But that was only the beginning. He held my hands behind my back and thrust into me over and over, harder and harder, then he reached one hand high in the air.

Slap!

I felt a stinging on my ass and then a sudden burst

of electric shock like I had never experienced in my life. It was as if I was being pierced through and through with a joy that I was almost unimaginable.

"Oh God!" I cried.

I didn't even have time to think. What was happening?

Slap!

He hit me again, even harder this time. The feeling was more intense than before. The stinging on my butt went straight to my pussy, which was throbbing and grasping at his cock with each slap.

Slap! Slap!

"Yes! Yes!" I shrieked.

I didn't care who heard me. I was in a universe of pleasure. The pain of Vinnie's hand slapping against my ass intensified the exquisite orgasms that his cock was delivering with each thrust into my pussy.

Orgasm!

I couldn't stop. I was begging for more and more. All I could think about was his hard cock slamming into my pussy and the slaps of his hand, harder and harder on my ass.

"Fuck me! FUCK ME!" I cried, and finally "SPANK ME!!"

With that, Vinnie thrust inside me deeper and harder than ever, grabbing my hips and slamming his cock into me, finally let out a loud cry and emptying himself deep inside me.

Orgasm.

"Ahhhh…"

It took a few minutes for me to recover enough to even talk. I picked up my skirt and blouse and slowly put them on as Vinnie watched me, devouring me with his eyes. I straightened my hair in the mirror and tried to put on some lipstick, but Vinnie interrupted me with a long, passionate kiss.

"Are you glad you came back?" he asked.

I smiled.

"That was incredible."

"Welcome to my world," he said with a smile.

I blushed a bit, but I knew exactly what he was saying. I never thought that my body could respond that way. And if somebody had said I would enjoy a guy spanking me, I would have thought they were crazy. But there I was, my pussy still throbbing from his amazing cock and my ass still stinging from the spanking. I was feeling the warm afterglow of incredible sex and everything about it felt right.

"I had no idea." I said.

"It's only the beginning," replied Vinnie.

I didn't know what to say. I had read his Rules and they had sort of scared me, but after what had just happened, I only wanted more. More of Vinnie, more spanking, more everything. I was ready to completely surrender myself to Mr. Vincent Griso, Junior. No matter what.

Vinnie must have sensed what I was thinking because he turned to me and asked:

"Are you ready to obey the Rules?"

I smiled and hesitated for a moment, just to add some suspense. But I didn't have any doubt at all.

"Yes, sir!"

He gave a laugh and threw his arms around me.

"Hooray!"

"Are you happy?" I asked.

"Very happy," he said.

And then he kissed me again, this time even longer and more intensely than before. I have never been happier in my whole life than I was right then.

Chapter Eleven

I have to say my butt was pretty sore the next day. And even though I had trouble sitting down and had to say hello to Mr. Ice Pack, I was in a state of bliss. All I could think about was Vinnie and how beautiful we were together. And even though it hurt when he spanked me, I was so caught up in the passion of the moment that even the stinging pain of his palm on my bare butt brought incredible pleasure.

"I can't believe your saying that!" said Shelly, as she sat on the couch watching me put another ice pack on my butt.

"But it's true, Shel. There was something really sexy about it."

"So what's next? Whips? Chains?"

"No," I said. "Just a little mild spanking. What's wrong with that?"

"It's sick, that's what's wrong with it."

"I didn't know you were such a prude, Shelly."

"I'm not a prude. But I'm not going to let some dude

spank my butt. It's demeaning."

"I guess. But it also feels kind of sexy."

"Not the next day it doesn't."

"True. Still, it kind of reminds me of him."

"I'm worried about you, Annabelle."

"Don't worry. I can take care of myself."

I think Shelly was a little jealous. After all, her boyfriend just sat around all day watching pornos on the couch. He didn't pay the least bit of attention to her. Maybe she was jealous of me and Vinnie – her boyfriend didn't even care enough to spank her. Plus, I think she was also a little bit curious about the whole spanking thing.

"So, what does it feel like exactly?"

"It's like...I turn myself over completely to him."

"And how does that feel?"

"Actually, kind of sexy."

"But what about the spanking part?"

"Okay, it kind of stings. But at the same time, it really turns me on. Do you think that's sick?"

Shelly paused, for a minute, giving this some thought.

"Maybe not. I guess I can sort of imagine it."

"Really, Shel?"

"Yeah. It's not like I'd go out looking for anything like that. But maybe under the right circumstances."

"That's what I'm saying. Vinnie is so sweet and soooo hot."

"And soooo rich!"

"That's true."

We both started giggling and ended up giving each other a big hug. I knew Shelly was my best friend forever and no matter what happened or what guy I went out with, we would still be friends.

"So, when are you moving into your new condo?"

"OhmyGod," I said. "I nearly forgot. I have to go pick out some furniture this afternoon."

"Is Vinnie going with you?"

"No. He doesn't care. He just told me to buy whatever I want."

"Must be nice," said Shelly with a sigh.

"Don't worry, Shel. You'll find somebody nice."

"Yeah, as soon as I get rid of Mr. Wonderful over there."

Her boyfriend, who had been watching pornos on the computer in the other room, poked his head in right then.

"You talkin' about me?" he asked.

"No," said Shelly, deadpan. "I was talkin' about Mr. Wonderful."

"Oh, yeah. And someday your fuckin' prince will come, right?"

"Fuck off," said Shelly flashing him the middle finger.

"Nice talk," said her boyfriend, and went back to his pornos.

That afternoon, I spent a couple of hours at the furniture store picking out a bedroom set and a dining room table. This was going to be my perfect dream house, so I made sure to pick out 1,000 thread-count sheets and really nice dishware. I didn't have of my own stuff, and Vinnie told me to buy whatever I wanted. So I did.

After shopping for furniture, I decided I needed to get going on my new wardrobe, so I went over to Macy's and picked out a couple of really nice tasteful outfits that were definitely sexy but not trashy. And I bought a few pair of shoes, including some new stiletto heels that were maybe a little trashy but also elegant and sexy. Vinnie said I should get a whole new wardrobe and shoes were definitely an essential. So I'm trying on like the fortieth pair of shoes when I get a text from Vinnie.

"Where r u?"

I smiled. He was thinking about me.

"Macys"
"Buying something sexy?"
"Yep."
"I want to see u"
"Ok. When?"
"Now"
"Where?"

"My office"

"Ok"

"15 mins"

"Yessir"

I smiled. I figured he'd like that last text. I was glad I'd bought some new shoes and outfits because I could change right there in the store and go right over to Vinnie's office. I was excited to see him, and also to show off my new clothes and shoes. I knew I'd have to hurry because Vinnie can be impatient, and I didn't want him to be upset. I made it from Macys to his office in exactly 14 minutes, and raced into the lobby of his building, carrying all my shopping bags.

The guard greeted me with a big smile.

"Good afternoon, Miss Stilletto."

"Good afternoon," I said cheerfully.

"You sure look nice," he said, admiring my new clothes.

"Why thank you," I replied, giving him a wink.

"I'll let Mr. Griso know you're here."

"Thanks"

I made my way to the elevator and up to the third floor. When the door opened, Vinnie's receptionist jumped up to greet me.

"Welcome, Miss Stilletto," she said.

"Hi."

I could tell that she was checking me out from head to toe, giving my new outfit the critical eye. I could also tell that she was way jealous of me. It was not only the new clothes, but also I had landed Vinnie Griso, her boss, the big fish. Eat your heart out, girl, I thought to myself as I gave her a big shit-eating grin.

"Mr. Griso is expecting you."

I bet he is.

As I followed her down the corridor into Vinnie's office, I checked myself out in a mirror on the way. I looked fabulous, if I did say so myself. I was excited to see Vinnie and show off my new outfit. I have to say, I was brimming with confidence. At least for me.

I wanted to make a big entrance into Vinnie's office, so I kind of swept through the door like I imagined somebody like Madonna or Lady Gaga might do.

"Hellllooo," I crowed, with a big smile, kind of swishing my hips and sticking my chest out.

Vinnie was at his desk. He didn't even look up.

"Hello?" I said, feeling let down.

"Come over here," said Vinnie, still not looking up at me.

I went over and stood quietly at his desk while he finished whatever he was doing. Finally, he looked up at me, kind of squinting as he checked out my outfit.

"Is that new?" he asked.

"Yeah," I said with a big grin. "Do you like it?"

He scowled.

"Not really."

I could feel myself starting to cry. But I held back. I didn't want to show Vinnie how upset I was.

"What's wrong with it?"

"It sucks."

"Really. I thought it was pretty."

"You were wrong."

Now I was definitely going to cry. But I was determined not to let Vinnie see me, so I started doing what I do when I'm nervous – bite the inside of my cheek.

Vinnie looked up at me again.

"Don't do that."

"Why not?"

"Because I said so."

I could tell the tears were already rolling down my cheeks, but I stopped biting my cheek anyway.

Vinnie looked at me again.

"Are you crying?"

"Yes."

"Why?"

"Because you are being mean."

"You think this is mean?"

"Yes."

"Well, it's not."

Right then I started to get angry.

"It sure as hell is. I spent a lot of time picking out

this outfit because I wanted to look great for you. And all you can say is 'It sucks?' You know how that makes me feel? Like a piece of shit. So if you don't like my taste in clothes, fine. You can take this back right now. I don't want it."

With that, I started taking off the blouse and skirt. I didn't care if I ripped them or anything. I was so mad at Vinnie, I didn't care if I never saw him again.

"What are you doing?"

I looked at him like he was a friggin' idiot.

"I'm giving you back your damn clothes."

"No, what are you doing?"

"What do you mean?"

He gave me a cold stare.

"Are you pissed off at me?"

"Shit yes?"

"Are you telling me I'm wrong about your outfit?"

"Uh....yeah."

"So you are disagreeing with me?"

"Definitely."

"As in disobeying me?"

I was finally beginning to get the drift of this conversation.

"Uh-huh," I said meekly.

"What do the Rules say about disobeying me?"

"I'm not supposed to disobey you."

"And if you do?"

"You....punish me."

"That's right," said Vinnie with a gleam in his eyes. "Are you ready to get punished?"

Definitely. In a matter of about ten seconds, I was already really turned on. I had taken off my blouse and skirt and was standing there half-naked.

"Yes," I said, with a big grin. "I am."

With that, Vinnie stood up from his desk, went over to the bookshelf, pulled out his copy of The Story of O, and the whole bookshelf swung open, leading to his Secret Room. In a flash, Vinnie had pulled me into the Secret Room and was ripping my clothes off – literally – he was tearing my new outfit to shreds. But I didn't care, I was so excited, even eager, for his punishment.

He pulled off my bra and my panties with a one swift tug and I was left naked and cowering – happily, I gotta say. Then he grabbed me by the wrists and pushed me up against the padded wall of the room, pressing himself against me so hard that I could feel his erect cock against my naked stomach.

Holding me tightly, he reached over and grabbed my right wrist and wrapped it around a velvet rope that was hanging against the wall. Then he took the other wrist and fastened it securely to another velvet rope. I was stretched out against the wall – naked, helpless and totally within his power.

Vinnie stood back and stared at me for a moment. He was looking adoringly at every part of my body, like I was this beautiful Greek goddess waiting to be ravished. That look of lust in his eyes was turning me to jelly. My body started to tingle and ache for him. I wanted nothing more than for this man to fuck me, now!

But Vinnie had some other ideas. He was going to torture me first. As he slowly took off his shirt and his pants, I watched him hungrily, thinking about his arms wrapped around me and his hard body thrusting into mine. Turning his back, he slowly pulled down his Calvin Kleins and I gazed at his firm athletic ass. Then he swiveled slightly to reveal his large, throbbing cock, reaching up as if it was beckoning me to plunge my pussy down onto it.

But I would have to wait. Vinnie moved slowly toward me, reaching over to gently touch my hard nipples with his tongue. I gasped as he licked them softly, then moaned as his tongue played across my neck and stomach. I longed to reach out, put my arms around him and pull him towards me, but my hands were firmly restrained. He knelt in front of me, reaching around to grab my ass, and his cock brushed gently against my thigh.

"Please," I moaned, wanting desperately to caress his cock with my fingers, my mouth, my pussy.

"Not yet," he murmured, as he softly parted my thighs.

"Ohmygod..." I gasped.

He began by licking the inside of my thighs, ever so slowly. It was torture as he ran his tongue almost up to the lips of my pussy, then stopped and began again. I would try to press my pussy against his mouth, but each time he pulled away. At last, he took his tongue and very slowly and deliberately ran it across the length of my pussy.

"Oh...oh..." I groaned, nearly faint with pleasure.

After a moment or two, while I was still breathless with excitement, Vinnie stood up and went over to a small desk. He opened the drawer and pulled out what looked with a tiny whip – made entirely of strands of tightly woven silk – which I later learned was called a "cat-of-nine-tails" He came back with the whip and, pulling my thighs even wider apart, he ran the soft silky whip along the length of my pussy.

I have never felt a sensation like that before. It was as if a thousand tiny tongues were licking at my pussy at the same time. It sent jolts of pleasure up and down my spine, and made me quiver with desire. I was aching to have Vinnie inside of me. Drawing the whip out from between my legs, Vinnie let the strands drape slowly across my tummy and my breasts. Then, with a quick flick of his wrist, he snapped the whip lightly across my taut nipples.

"Ohhhh..." I moaned. It was wisp of pain mixed with pleasure, leaving me wanting more.

Snap.

He flicked the tiny whip harder this time, intensifying the pain, but increasing the pleasure.

"Yes, yes..."

He smiled and whipped me harder.

Snap!

This time the flash of pain rippled all the way down my body, inside and out.

"More..." I whispered, despite myself.

I looked up at Vinnie. He was smiling a broad happy grin. If anything, his cock had grown bigger and even more erect.

"Not yet," he whispered back to me.

This time he went over and opened a small bar. He searched inside the bar and came back with an ice cube in his hand. It looked like it had been molded for a very special purpose that I was soon to discover. First, he brushed it lightly against my nipples, sending a chill through my body that added to the intensity of my excitement. Then he ran the ice cube slowly down my stomach to my pussy, where he drew it slowly up and down the lips, sending shivers over my whole body. He teased it gently against my clit, which made my brain feel like it was about to explode, then he pulled the lips of my pussy apart and slid the ice cube slowly inside me – which made me feel like I was turned inside out with pleasure.

"Fire and ice," murmured Vinnie, almost to himself.

I was almost too wrapped up in this cycle of pain and pleasure to even hear him. But I watched as he took a long red candle from the candelabra near the desk, lit it and brought it over to me.

OhmyGod, I thought to myself. Is he going to burn me? I was suddenly frightened, and struggled against the velvet ropes, but I couldn't get free.

"What are you going to do?" I pleaded.

"You'll see," Vinnie said with an almost demonic grin.

He held the candle near my body, gazing at me as it cast a golden light over my flesh – my breasts, my face, my stomach, my hips.

"You are so beautiful," he murmured.

I was relishing the adoration, but I was still scared about what might happen as I struggled – bound, naked and helpless.

"Don't be afraid," said Vinnie. Something in the tone of his voice reassured me, but I still was very scared about what might happen.

As the candle burned, he held it for a long moment over my stomach. After a few second, a drip of hot wax dribbled onto my stomach.

"Owwww!" I cried out in pain.

Immediately, Vinnie leaned over and kissed my stomach to ease my pain. As he kissed me, the burning turned to the warmth of desire. Somewhere deep inside of me, I wanted more.

Vinnie sensed this, and lifted the candle up over my breasts. I closed my eyes, afraid to watch. After an excruciating moment of suspense, the hot wax dripped down on my nipple.

"Aiiieee" I screamed.

Again, Vinnie bent over and kissed me, sucking gently on my nipple. The warmth of the hot wax and the passion of his kisses melted all the pain away and transformed it into splendid pleasure. Soon, he turned to the other nipple, and again I was moaning with a mix of pain and pleasure. More than anything, I was aching to have his cock deep inside my pussy.

"Fuck me. Please fuck me..." I begged.

Vinnie smiled and blew out the candle. Then he took the candle and traced a line down from my breasts to my stomach and my thighs. Slowly he parted the lips of my pussy, which was dripping wet, and slid the candle along the outside, then pushed it gently inside as he lightly teased my clit with his finger. I could feel my pussy clenching against the soft, smooth candle even as my clit was pulsating with excitement. As Vinnie flicked my clit and slid the candle in and out of my pussy, all my pent-up passion and desire exploded.

Orgasm.

"Don't stop, don't stop..." I groaned as he thrust the candle deeper and harder into me, all the while caressing my clit with his finger.

"Ohgod..." I moaned. "Fuck me...please! Please!!"

Vinnie stood up quickly and spun me around so that one arm was splayed behind my back. He spread my legs apart wide as he thrust his cock up against my ass, then ran it up and down my soaking pussy lips.

"Please..." I begged. "Put it in me."

In a single thrust, he rammed his cock inside me. I nearly screamed with joy as my hungry pussy engulfed him.

Snap!

I felt the strands of the silk whip slapping across my ass and Vinnie drove himself deeper inside.

"Oh, yes, yes!" I was practically shrieking now. "Fuck me. Fuck me!!"

Orgasm!

I was coming hard now, pushing myself against Vinnie as he began to groan with passion, slapping my ass harder and harder with the whip.

Snap!! Snap!!

Pain and pleasure melted into one as I surrendered every ounce of my flesh to Vinnie. He was pumping himself so deep inside me it felt like I was suffocating.

"OhGod!" he cried, spilling all his seed into me in a gripping burst of passion.

After a moment, he pulled away. He kissed me gently and slowly untied me from the velvet ropes. I could barely stand, my knees were so wobbly. As I looked up at Vinnie, I thought I saw his eyes fill with tears. My heart suddenly felt like it was leaping out of my chest. I wanted to hug him and comfort him and, yes, love him forever. But, at that moment, I knew I couldn't say anything.

Chapter Twelve

The next few weeks were pretty much utter bliss. I moved into my new condo – furnished, of course, by Vinnie's interior decorator. I didn't want to take any more chances by picking out the wrong furniture, although the punishment was pretty fun. Plus Vinnie got me a wardrobe consultant who helped me find exactly the right outfits. I have to admit, they actually looked great on me. And I loved my new red Mustang convertible. I drove it down to my old neighborhood in Jersey City so everybody could see how fabulous I looked. Even the stupid punks on the corner were speechless.

Shelly cried when I moved out of the apartment. I don't know if she was crying because she was sad to see me go or whether she was crying because she was stuck in that dumpy apartment with her doofus boyfriend while I was moving into a brand new condo paid for by my rich, hot boyfriend. Of course, she still disapproved of Vinnie and thought he was a sick weirdo, but some people are just narrow-minded and would never understand.

As for my mother and Aunt Dolores, I pretty much kept them in the dark about me and Vinnie. But, being a mother, she kind of suspected what was going on and invited me over one night for a "talk." Dolores was there, too, just to add her two cents.

"So tell us about this new boyfriend of yours."

I felt like it was going to be the Spanish Inquistion or something.

"He's very nice."

"And rich?"

"Yeah, he's rich."

"Vinnie's Auto Parts. I heard of them," chimed in Aunt Dolores. "Big money."

"So," asks my mother, "Are you his mistress or what?"

"No way, Ma. Vinnie's my boyfriend."

"Some boyfriend. He puts you up in a brand new condo five minutes from his office. Buys you clothes and a new car. Sounds like a mistress to me."

"You don't understand anything, Ma."

"I understand a lot, missy. So is he married?

"No."

"Divorced?"

"He's never been married."

"Is he gay?" piped up Aunt Dolores.

I had to laugh.

"No. He is definitely not gay."

"Then what's his problem?" said my mother with a

sneer.

"He doesn't have a problem, okay? Maybe he just likes me."

"Likes you is one thing. Buying you all that stuff is another thing all together."

"Ma, he likes me. And he's rich. So he buys me stuff."

"So what does he get?"

"Me," I snapped back.

"Well, I beg your pardon," she huffed.

My mother knew I was hiding things from her, and I did feel kinda guilty about it. But what was I supposed to tell her? That I was in an S&M relationship with this really cute, hot guy? And that it was actually this incredible feeling that I'd never had before? I didn't think she would ever understand.

After talking to my mom and Aunt Dolores, I started thinking more about my relationship with Vinnie. It's true, it was all about sex, at least on the surface. But I also knew that we had this powerful chemistry, and even though it might seem weird to someone on the outside, we were developing a real relationship, like nothing I'd ever had before. So I decided to talk to Shelly about it. I went over to her place and we sat outside on the stoop and talked. She smoked a cigarette – I didn't, since Vinnie didn't allow it.

"So are you falling in love with him?" she asked pointedly.

"No."

"I don't believe you."

"I'm not sure. I don't know."

"So you are."

"Kind of. Not exactly. I mean, he's so gorgeous, and he treats me really nice. Except when he doesn't. It's confusing."

"I'll say. You're walking around half the time with a sore butt. I don't call that nice."

"You don't understand."

"No, I guess I don't."

"It's like when I'm with him, I feel safe. Taken care of."

"Even though he beats the crap out of you?"

"But I want him to."

"You do?"

"I know it sounds nuts, but there is something about surrendering to him completely that really turns me on. It's like I'm giving myself over to his pleasure...and mine."

"You're right. I don't get it."

"It's like he's a little boy, and this is the only way he knows how to show love."

"Ouch."

"Yeah. Exactly."

"So are you going to tell him?"

"Tell him what?"

"How you feel about him."

I suddenly was flushed with fear at even the thought of telling Vinnie how I felt.

"No, I couldn't do that."

"Why not?"

"It would be against the Rules."

"Not that Rules shit again."

"It's not shit, Shelly. It's the Rules."

"How come you have to have Rules?"

"Because..."

I stopped myself. I realized I had never really thought about that. From the moment I agreed to follow Vinnie's Rules, I never questioned them. His Rules became my Rules. And there was no questioning them. That was all there was to it. But talking like this to Shelly made me think about things again. Was Vinnie always right? Did I always have to obey his Rules? And what if I was really falling in love with him?

The next day Vinnie invited me to his mansion for dinner. Since that first night, I had not been back there. He always had me come to his office or else would meet me at my new condo. So I thought it was a good sign that he was asking me back to his mansion. Of course, I had some bad memories from that night, but I figured maybe this was an important step in our relationship. Maybe he felt more comfortable with my being there, even after what happened with his mom and everything. Maybe, just maybe, this was the beginning of a new, deeper phase of our relationship.

I picked out Vinnie's favorite outfit and spent extra time on my makeup. When T-Bomb arrived to pick me up in the limo, I could tell he was wowed by how great I looked.

"Looking fine tonight, Miss Stilletto."

"Thank you, T."

As I settled into the back seat of the limo, sipping champagne, I started dreaming about me and Vinnie and what our future might be together. Okay, it wasn't exactly a normal relationship, but I knew I was falling in love with him, and I had this sixth sense that he felt the same way about me. It wasn't like I wanted to get married right away or anything, but it seemed like now was the time to tell him my real feelings. Sure, I was nervous about it, but excited at the same time.

When we got to the mansion, Vinnie greeted me with a big kiss and led me into the dining room for dinner. He was always getting me to try new food, so we had something called Cock Quills Saint Jock, which turned out to be these sort of fish balls called scallops. Normally, I would never eat stuff like that, so I think Vinnie got a kick out of seeing whether I would gag or not. Fortunately, they didn't taste too bad, although I like fish sticks better than those scallop dealies.

We went through a couple of bottles of wine between us, so I was pretty damn drunk by the end of dinner. I kept wanting to have "The Talk" with him during dinner, but I could never find the right time. Plus, during the whole meal, he was looking at me like he wanted to fuck me right there on the table, but of course Stewart the butler was there so we couldn't exactly make love right in the middle of dinner.

Afterwards, we went into Vinnie's Secret Room and started going at it hot and heavy. He had tied me up facing the wall with those velvet ropes and was giving me a real good spanking. I was very turned on, as usual, and I could feel how aroused Vinnie was as he pressed his cock against my ass. But when he turned me around to face him with the cat-of-nine-tails in one hand and a wooden paddle in the other, I decided that I couldn't go any further before we had "The Talk." Okay, maybe it wasn't the best timing in the world, but all I could think about was me and Vinnie and our relationship and the future. And that was starting to get in the way of my enjoyment of sex.

"Vinnie," I said as he rubbed the cat-of-nine-tails against my pussy.

"What?" he said breathlessly.

"We have to talk.'

"About what?"

"Me and you. Us."

"Now?"

"Yeah, I feel like we need to talk."

"Jesus, Annabelle..."

"I'm sorry, but I have to talk to you."

He looked at me sternly.

"You know this is totally against the Rules."

"I know," I sighed.

"You could get punished really bad for this."

"I know."

That seemed to cheer Vinnie up a little.

"Okay," he said and put down the cat-of-nine-tails and paddle. I could see his erection wilting at the same time. "So what do you want to talk about?"

"About us."

"What about us?"

Now I was getting really nervous. I didn't quite know what to say, or how to say it. And Vinnie looked like he might get real mad.

"Well....uh..."

"What?"

"You know, you and me have been doing this for awhile now."

"Doing what?"

"Uh....this."

"Okay."

"And I feel really good about what we've been doing."

"Me, too. So what's the problem?"

"There's not a problem. It's just that...I've been thinking..."

"Yes?"

I was totally nervous now and was hyperventilating and, of course, chewing on my cheek.

"Don't do that," said Vinnie.

"Sorry, " I mumbled.

"I mean it."

I could see he did. Whenever I chewed on my cheek, he got totally turned on. I noticed his dick was getting hard again. I thought about forgetting about the whole "Talk" thing, but decided I had to keep going. I couldn't just let it drop like that.

"Okay," I continued, "I've been thinking about how happy you've made me."

"I want you to be happy," said Vinnie.

"I know. And you've bought me all these wonderful things and treated me so nice. It's just that..."

"What?"

"I think I'm kind of....sort of....falling for you."

"What do you mean?" said Vinnie. He had this look of shock on his face.

"Well, we have this great chemistry and we get along so good and you make me so happy. I couldn't help myself."

"Are you saying...?"

"Yeah. I'm in love with you, Vinnie."

Vinnie stared at me with a look of total shock.

"Holy shit!"

"What's wrong?"

"You realize this is totally against the Rules."

"There wasn't anything in the Rules about this."

"Yeah, but it goes against everything in the Rules. It's like...it was understood."

My heart was sinking real fast. I felt like I was going to pass out.

"It wasn't 'understood' by me."

"Well, maybe you should have thought about it some more before you agreed."

"How was I supposed to think about it? I didn't expect to fall in love with you."

"You can't fall in love with me, Annabelle. You just can't."

Vinnie had a look of desperation on his face. He was almost pleading with me.

"I can't help myself, Vinnie. I can't control my feelings."

"But...this could ruin everything."

"Why? Because you don't feel the same way about me?"

"I can't, Annabelle. I just can't."

"Why not?"

"It's hard to explain. But I'm not built that way. It's impossible."

"Nothing is impossible."

"This is."

"Vinnie, I love you. And I believe you love me too. Why is that impossible?"

"Because it breaks all the Rules."

"And your Rules are so damned important?"

"Yes. You know they are."

"Well, you know what? You can go fuck your Rules. Because you're not going to be fucking me anymore."

"Annabelle, please..."

I grabbed my clothes from the floor and started hurriedly dressing.

"I don't want to see you anymore, Vinnie. You can take back your car and your condo and all the nice clothes you bought me. Because I'm not going to be playing by your Rules anymore."

"Annabelle...."

By this time, I was almost dressed and rushed for the door.

"I don't want to talk about it. And I don't want to see you again, ever."

At that, I stormed out the door of Vinnie's Secret Room and slammed it behind me. With tears streaming down my face, I hopped into the limo and had T-Bomb drive me home. I sobbed all the way.

Epilogue

For the next few weeks, I tried to get my life back to normal. I moved out of the condo, sold my red Mustang, but I kept the new clothes Vinnie had bought me. I moved back into the apartment with Shelly, who was glad I was back, although I think she missed hearing about all my sexual exploits with Vinnie. I had gone from her inexperienced friend to Miss Adventure, which must have spiced up her fantasy life quite a bit. I didn't hear from Vinnie for a day or two after that night at his mansion, but then he started texting me.

"I miss u."
"Please come back."
"I want to see u. now."

I ignored the texts for awhile, even as Vinnie began to sound more desperate.

"I need u. bad."

"Don't leave me"

"Waaahhhh!!"

I had to smile at that last one. He was like a little kid who had his candy taken away. But I was more than a piece of eye candy – or maybe cock candy. I had feelings for Vinnie, and if he couldn't admit his feelings for me, then I wasn't going to be involved with him anymore. I was worth more than that. A lot more.

"Don't answer him," said Shelly.

And I didn't. At least for awhile.

Then he sent me one more text:

"Can we have coffee?"

That sounded pretty harmless. And by that time, I thought I could see him without completely falling apart.

"Okay. When?"

"Today. 3. Busters?"

Busters was a little coffee shop near his office. Quiet. Safe. So I agreed.

"Ok"

T-Bomb picked me up and drove me to the coffee shop. I hadn't tried to get real dressed up or to look sexy or anything. I figured it was best for Vinnie to see me how I really am without any of the pretense. When I got to the coffee shop, he was waiting there, sipping on a latte. He looked as gorgeous as ever in his tight black pants and pointy shoes. My heart leapt for a moment when he looked up at me with those clear blue eyes, even though we could never go back to that moment when we first met.

"Hi," he said softly.

"Hi."

"Please sit down."

"Thanks."

There was an awkward moment as we stared at each other. My mind was filled with all the images of us together – the sweat and passion, the tenderness, the pain and the pleasure. He was probably thinking about the same things.

"Would you like some coffee?"

"No thanks. I'm good."

Somehow I wanted to keep this meeting as simple as possible.

"How have you been?" asked Vinnie.

"Good. And you?"

"I'm okay."

I was expecting him to say how much he missed me and how he couldn't possibly live without me. I was disappointed, but I also sensed a deep sadness from him, which I had not seen before.

"I wanted to tell you how sorry I was," he said. "About everything."

"It's okay."

"No. I was wrong."

"No, you weren't. It was what I wanted, too."

"I don't mean about the Rules and all that. When you told me about your feelings, I shouldn't have treated you that way."

"Don't worry. I understand."

"Do you?"

I nodded.

"I think so."

"I wish I did. I wish I knew why I am the way I am. And I wish I could change everything about myself. But I can't."

"You know what? You shouldn't change a thing. You're wonderful just the way you are."

"Except that I can't allow anyone to love me."

I didn't know what to say to that. It was true. But I guess there was nothing either one of us could do about it.

We sat in silence for what seemed like a long time. Finally, he looked up at me.

"I have something for you."

"You don't have to."

"Yes, I do."

He reached into his pocket and pulled out a small blue box. Tiffany's, of course. I couldn't help hyperventilating a bit.

"Here," he held the box out to me.

"No, Vinnie, I can't."

"Please?"

I was torn. If I accepted the gift, would it mean

that he expected something in return? Shelly had warned me that he would do anything to get me back, and a little blue box from Tiffany's was a pretty good start. Still, I had a feeling that this was a gift that came with no strings attached. Straight from Vinnie's heart, if that was possible.

I took the box and, with my hands shaking, I opened it. Inside was a beautiful gold and diamond-encrusted necklace with two intertwined hearts. My eyes filled with tears.

"Oh, Vinnie. It's beautiful."

"Not as beautiful as you."

"Thank you," I said, brushing away the tears. "For this, and for everything."

"I'm the one who should be thanking you," he said.

We talked for a few more minutes, then he had to leave for a business meeting. He helped me put on the necklace and then kissed me gently on the cheek before he left. As I watched him walk out the door and disappear, I wondered if I would ever see him again. I knew that Vinnie had changed my life, and I believed he had changed mine. And I knew that I still loved him, even if love was impossible for him. Or was it? Would it ever be possible for him to love someone the way I loved him? For now, I struggled to put that lingering question out of my mind. "Only time will tell," as my Aunt Dolores would say. "Only time will tell."

Lightning Source UK Ltd.
Milton Keynes UK
UKOW051822230812

197994UK00001B/92/P